She was he[...]

Warm and al[...] [...]n with a fierceness [...] [...]is body to stand at attention.

He knew he should push her away, but he was incapable of breaking the delicious contact.

Every fantasy he'd ever had of Holly Durant—and he'd had more than his share—was playing out in front of him, and he wasn't about to do anything to ruin it. He couldn't breathe. Couldn't think straight. Desire slammed into him, fierce and hard. Sweet Christ, she was the most gorgeous woman he had ever seen.

The microscopic part of his brain that still functioned was firing warning shots. He was all wrong for her.

"Holly," he finally said, his voice strained and thick. "We can't do this."

But she only moved closer. "Yes, we can," she contradicted him softly, pressing a moist kiss against his collarbone.

To hell with doing what was right. Nothing could prevent him from reaching for Holly, not even the sound of his cane as it clattered onto the floor. The warning shots had come too late; he'd just taken a direct hit and he was going down....

Blaze

Dear Reader,

It seems just yesterday that I was sitting with my editor, brainstorming ideas for this exciting miniseries, which revolves around four soldiers and how each of their lives is altered by the events of a single day. And suddenly, here I am, writing the final book.

I loved coming up with the heroine of this story. Lt. Holly Durant is so strong and never wavers in going after what she wants, even if it means risking enemy fire to save the man she loves. Holly is hailed as a hero for her actions, but it's up to Sgt. Shane Rafferty to keep her safe when the enemy follows her home.

I hope you enjoy reading Holly and Shane's story as they discover the true meaning of what it takes to be a hero!

Happy reading!

Karen Foley

Karen Foley

HEAT OF THE MOMENT

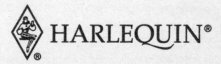

HARLEQUIN®

TORONTO • NEW YORK • LONDON
AMSTERDAM • PARIS • SYDNEY • HAMBURG
STOCKHOLM • ATHENS • TOKYO • MILAN • MADRID
PRAGUE • WARSAW • BUDAPEST • AUCKLAND

Recycling programs
for this product may
not exist in your area.

ISBN-13: 978-0-373-79600-7

HEAT OF THE MOMENT

ABOUT THE AUTHOR

Karen Foley is an incurable romantic. When she's not watching romantic movies, she's writing sexy romances with strong heroes and happy endings. She lives in Massachusetts with her husband and two daughters, and enjoys hearing from her readers. You can find out more about her by visiting www.karenefoley.com.

Books by Karen Foley

HARLEQUIN BLAZE
353—FLYBOY
422—OVERNIGHT SENSATION
451—ABLE-BODIED
504—HOLD ON TO THE NIGHTS
549—BORN ON THE 4TH OF JULY
    "Packing Heat"
563—HOT-BLOODED

For Lt. Col. Kathy Lauden, Maj. Kristi Lowenthal,
and Lt. Erika "Mo" Schoenthal;
your selflessness and dedication are an
inspiration. Thank you for your service.

1

NAVY LIEUTENANT HOLLY Durant blew out a hard breath of frustration and glanced into the passenger mirror of the five ton cargo truck. The five or six days that it would take to complete this particular assignment meant that the mountain of paperwork waiting for her back at Al Asad Air Base would be twice as high when she returned. At this rate, she'd never catch up.

Behind her, a convoy of military supply vehicles stretched for a quarter of a mile along the dusty road. She didn't typically accompany the movement of supplies to the outlying posts, but this assignment was unique. She was personally escorting her senior supply clerk, Sergeant Ramon Martinez, from Al Asad Air Base to Camp Fallujah, a forward operating base located a hundred kilometers away. She no longer trusted him with the responsibility of overseeing the massive supply operations in Iraq. At Camp Fallujah, he would work under the direct supervision of a senior officer in supplying repair parts and construction equipment to the

Seabees in western Iraq. Technically, it wasn't a demotion, but she was sure he didn't see it that way. A quiet man by nature, he'd been even more so during the two hours that they'd been driving together.

Her gaze slid sideways toward the sergeant, noting the sheen of sweat that coated his skin. As if sensing her silent appraisal, he turned his dark eyes to her and Holly had to push down her own misgivings and feelings of guilt about having initiated an investigation into his activities. He had the largest, most expressive eyes she had ever seen on a man, and right now they reminded her of a dog that had just been kicked. He obviously didn't understand why he was being moved to a new location and Holly couldn't tell him the truth. She'd merely told him that Fallujah needed an experienced supply clerk, but his unhappiness was apparent in the defeated slump of his shoulders, and the way he repeatedly sighed.

"If you're getting tired, we can switch at the next turnoff and I can drive," she offered, although she knew he would refuse. Despite her suspicions, Sgt. Martinez was unfailingly polite and respectful of her rank.

His eyes widened. "Oh, no. I'm fine driving, ma'am. But thank you for the offer."

Holly nodded and turned her attention away. Maybe she should have confronted him directly. Maybe, after all, there was a reasonable explanation for what was going on. It was difficult to imagine the mild-mannered sergeant was capable of any wrongdoing. But it was too late; she had already initiated an investigation into the supply process at Al Asad and now it was up to the Inspector General to determine if any crime had been committed.

Holly suspected that Martinez was responsible for the loss of tens of thousands and maybe even hundreds of thousands of dollars worth of supplies, but she had no solid proof. Although his job required that he obtain receipts for the equipment he received and sent out, he consistently had excuses and explanations for why he hadn't acquired the requisite documentation, or why the paperwork he did have was sloppy and full of errors. He also had access to a substantial fund of money with which to procure certain supplies and services from local contractors, rather than going through the protracted process of waiting for the items to be shipped from the States.

Holly had begun the task of reconciling these accounts, but it would take her weeks to sort through the thousands of transactions. Constructing buildings, repairing runways, and maintaining an infrastructure in such a remote and inhospitable location was hard enough without somebody deliberately sabotaging their efforts. That one of her men might be responsible was intolerable, and although she found it difficult to imagine Martinez doing anything so sleazy, all the evidence indicated otherwise.

She'd voiced her suspicions to her commanding officer, Commander Comstock, several weeks ago. He'd assured her that he would look into the matter, but when she'd broached the subject to him again, just days earlier, he'd been uncharacteristically short with her. He'd curtly told her that he didn't need a lieutenant to tell him how to do his job, and that the situation was being handled. Whatever that meant.

So Holly had filed a hotline complaint with the Inspector General of the Navy—a brief description of what she believed was going on, including the estimated dollar loss—that very morning. She wasn't sure what would happen, but knew she risked a reprimand from Commander Comstock if it turned out that he had already initiated an investigation of his own.

Holly knew Sgt. Martinez was upset about the transfer to Camp Fallujah, but moving him was the right thing to do. Until an investigation cleared him of any wrongdoing, she wanted him where he could do the least amount of damage.

In the side mirror, Holly thought she glimpsed one of the reinforced gun trucks that had been assigned to protect the convoy. Just knowing that Gunnery Sergeant Shane Rafferty was manning that machine gun gave her a sense of comfort. She liked knowing he was close by, in case she needed him.

In case he needed *her,* although he'd never acknowledge such a thing might be possible. Shane Rafferty was six feet, two inches of solid, honed muscle and testosterone, and she couldn't imagine him ever admitting that he needed anyone. Especially her.

Well, except for that single night three years ago in the guest room over her parents' boathouse, when he'd finally given up all pretenses. For that one night, he had been completely hers and Holly had been blown away by his intensity. For that one night she'd actually allowed herself to hope that he might reciprocate the feelings she had for him. But when morning had come, he'd been gone. He'd returned to active duty without even saying goodbye and try as she might, Holly had been unable to get over him.

For a moment, she let her mind drift back to when she'd first met Shane, ten years earlier. She'd been fifteen years old when he and his father had moved into the three-room apartment over Benjamin's Drugstore. There had been rumors about his family: his father was a drunk and his mother had run off with another man. In the small, wealthy town of Chatham, Virginia, Shane Rafferty had stood out like a common weed in a garden of roses. He didn't even attend the public high school in town—Holly had heard whisperings that he'd dropped out before he'd come to Chatham. Holly would probably never have crossed paths with him except that at seventeen, he was the same age as her brother, Mitch. Mitch attended the prestigious Hargrave Military Academy, but he'd worked with Shane at the drugstore on the weekends. Despite the differences in their backgrounds, they had become good friends.

During that year and the following summer, before Mitch had left for college and Shane had enlisted in the Marines, Shane had spent more time hanging out at her home than he did at his own, which hadn't bothered Holly at all. She'd attended Chatham Hall, a private all-girls boarding school in town, and while the school hosted dances and other social activities with the boys from Hargrave Academy, none of those boys had been as fascinating to Holly as Shane Rafferty had been, with his knowing eyes and leanly muscled physique.

But more than his physical appeal, his total aloneness had attracted Holly. She sensed that Shane resented having to depend on anyone for anything. If the rumors were to be believed, he certainly couldn't depend on his father. In fact, it had appeared that Shane took care of his dad, and not the other way around. He'd worked full-time at the drugstore, and Holly had seen him at the Food Lion on several occasions, buying real groceries and not just junk food. It was no wonder he hadn't mixed well with the snooty boys from Hargrave; he was worlds away from their entitled, finely choreographed lifestyles. He might hang out with her brother, but Holly guessed that even Mitch wasn't allowed full access to Shane's innermost thoughts or secrets.

Holly thought it must get tiring, always having to be so strong and responsible. She wanted him to see that he didn't always need to be so separate and alone. She ached to take some of the burden from his shoulders; to let him know that he could lean on her, even just a little. That he could let her love him, even just a little.

Her parents had bought her a camera for her birthday, and she'd enrolled in a photography class at Chatham Hall. She'd carried that camera with her everywhere and had taken furtive photos of Shane whenever she had the chance. Her favorite was a picture of him sleeping on the hammock by the lake, arms bent behind his head and his face turned slightly to one side. With his eyes closed and his mouth relaxed, he'd actually looked peaceful, with none of the bristling wariness he exhibited when he was awake.

But he'd completely ignored Holly, making it clear he had no interest in her. In fact, if Holly hadn't known better, she might have believed he went out of his way to avoid being alone with her, or having to talk to her.

The more he'd ignored her, the more she'd been determined to make him aware of her. She knew he wanted her; she'd caught him watching her when he thought she wasn't looking and the raw heat in his eyes had both terrified and thrilled her. But no matter how she'd tried to get close to him, he'd kept her at a distance. But a year later he'd enlisted in the military and he'd left without a backward glance. She hadn't seen him again for two years, when he had come home for the winter holidays. Mitch was home from college for several weeks, so her parents had invited Shane to spend Christmas Eve with them. She'd been almost eighteen and a senior in high school by then, and seeing Shane again had brought all the emotions of her earlier infatuation rushing back.

He'd looked different than she remembered, leaner and harder and more serious. She'd changed, too. She'd been little more than a child when he'd left. But since then, she'd filled out nicely and had perfected the art of flirtation. She could have had any of the boys at Hargrave Academy, but she'd wanted Shane. So she'd deliberately set out to entice and seduce him, never imagining that he might not welcome her advances.

Remembering that holiday week still caused Holly to cringe with embarrassment. She'd been so young and arrogant; so sure of her own appeal. On Christmas Eve, when her father had sent Shane down to the wine cellar to retrieve several more bottles for dinner, Holly had followed him. She'd launched a full frontal attack on him and for several long, blissful moments, she'd had Shane Rafferty right where she wanted him…up against the wall with her hands under his shirt, stroking his warm, hard muscles as he'd stood stiff and unresponsive.

He'd resisted for about five seconds before he'd all but consumed her, and the heat and intensity of his passion had left her breathless and shaken. If her father hadn't hollered down the stairs, she had no doubt what would have happened in that small basement room. But the interruption had given Shane time to regroup. He'd thrust her away and gathered up the bottles of wine.

"This never happened," he'd growled, his voice low

and rough. "I'm not what you want, and I'm definitely not what you need, so play your games with someone your own age. Just stay the hell away from me."

Holly had been both stunned and mortified by his reaction, and it had taken several long moments before she'd composed herself enough to return upstairs and sit down to dinner. Her brother had cast speculative looks at both of them, but if he'd noticed her flushed features or Shane's grim expression, he'd made no comment.

After that, Holly hadn't been able to stop thinking about him. If anything, their encounter in the wine cellar had only intensified her obsession with him. She'd been prepared for the same awkward fumbling and uncertainty she'd experienced with the boys she'd dated, but there had been none of that with Shane. His touch had been sure and confident, and she'd been the one to feel like a novice.

She'd thought of him constantly. They were perfect for each other. Nothing could convince her otherwise. She was meant to be with Shane Rafferty. She'd guessed that he considered her to be spoiled and shallow, but she'd prove to him otherwise. Until that moment, she hadn't planned on a military career for herself. She'd thought she would pursue a career in photography. But if joining the military would bring her closer to Shane, that's what she would do. So she'd joined ROTC and tried to squelch her feelings of guilt when her father had expressed his surprise and delight over her career choice. Personally, she had no doubts that she would do well in the Navy, but she knew that her father wouldn't approve of her real reasons for joining. But she needed to show Shane that she was more than just a pretty face. The military might not be her first career choice, but she'd make a good officer. And someday, if her plans worked out, a good military wife.

He'd come over to the house several more times during his holiday leave, and although he'd tried to avoid her, Holly had noticed how he would stiffen when she came too close, as if he barely held himself in check. She'd suspected that if she persisted, she could push past his restraint. More than anything, she'd wanted Shane to be her first, but she'd also known that the ensuing guilt he'd feel would drive him away, maybe forever. And so she'd waited.

Shane had come home with her brother one last time, to help celebrate her graduation from the Naval Academy. Despite the fact that her brother was an officer in the Navy while Shane was an enlisted man in the Marine Corps, the two men had remained friends. Her parents had thrown a party for her at their lake house in the foothills of the Blue Ridge Mountains, and Holly had been both shocked and delighted to see Shane. Admittedly, she'd had a little more to drink that night than she was accustomed to. Her only excuse was that his presence had caught her completely off guard, and she'd been acutely aware of him watching her the entire night. Four years had passed since her first inexpert attempt at seducing him, but she'd learned a thing or two about men since then.

The alcohol, combined with the expression in his eyes whenever she looked at him, had given her the courage she needed to launch a sensual assault on him, and this time he hadn't been able to resist. But when she'd woken up in his bed the next morning, she'd been alone. Shane had left without so much as a good-bye.

Sgt. Martinez downshifted, the deep growl of the

diesel engine pulling Holly out of her reverie. They were approaching a small village of mud huts, and Holly frowned as she noted the empty street. She made a small noise of concern and leaned forward to peer through the windshield, her hands gripping her M4 rifle.

"It's too quiet," Martinez observed, echoing Holly's thoughts. "I hope that doesn't mean trouble."

"I see some kids up ahead," Holly replied, nodding toward a group of children playing alongside the road just before the village. "That's a good sign, right?"

They rumbled slowly through the village, following behind the lead truck and the two Humvees assigned to provide security to the convoy. Aside from the children, there was no other indication of life in the village, and the hairs on the back of Holly's neck prickled uneasily.

They passed the children, who stopped to stare at them, and Holly told herself that the foreboding she felt was nothing more than her imagination. Reaching under her seat for her camera, she snapped several quick shots, capturing the awe in their big, dark eyes. Holding her camera and taking pictures gave her a sense of comfort, but as they drove through an orchard just beyond the village, she thought she saw something move deep in the shadowed recesses of the trees. Suddenly, there was a brilliant flash, followed by a deafening explosion. An instant later, the lead Humvee shot into the air and came down on its roof, completely engulfed in flames. The camera slipped from Holly's fingers and landed on the floor at her feet, forgotten.

"Goddamn! We're under attack!" Sgt. Martinez screamed.

"Pull over, pull over!"

He wrenched the wheel hard to the right, dragging the vehicle to a shuddering stop. Behind them, the convoy split into two lines, one on either side of the road, even as a second rocket-propelled grenade streaked out of the orchard and struck the supply truck directly in front of them, flipping the vehicle onto its side and sending molten fragments of metal high into the air.

Almost simultaneously, Holly heard the unmistakable spit of small arms fire, and realized they were being attacked from both sides of the road. Glancing through the passenger window, she saw that insurgents were firing at them from the orchard on one side, and a crudely dug trench on the other. Their forward position in the convoy made them a vulnerable target.

"We've got to get out of the truck," she gasped, and reached for her door handle.

Martinez looked at her in horror. "Are you kidding? It's not safe. We'll be killed out there!"

"It's not safe here," Holly insisted hotly. "We're directly in the kill zone! We stand a better chance if we move toward the rear vehicles."

The other soldier blanched, his dark eyes expressing his fear. "I'm a supply clerk. I'm not trained for combat!"

"You're a soldier," Holly said grimly, pushing down her own rising fear. "You've been trained for this, and you can do it. Now move! That's an order!"

Opening her door, Holly used it as a shield to survey her surroundings. The air was heavy and acrid with the stench of burning fuel and scorched metal. On the road behind her, the gun trucks were spraying both the trees and the trench with automatic gunfire. They'd formed two columns of vehicles on either side of the road, turning the road itself into a safe zone of sorts. Still, there were twenty yards of open space between Holly and that protected corridor, in which she and Sgt. Martinez would be completely vulnerable.

The noise of the battle was deafening, but Holly scarcely heard anything over the roar of her own frantic heartbeat. Shane was on top of one of those gun trucks. Her heart clenched hard at the thought of anything happening to him. In the next instant she reminded herself that he was a seasoned soldier—a hardened Marine. He'd been doing this for eight years and he could take care of himself. Her only concern now was to get herself and her supply clerk to safety.

She motioned for Martinez. "Stay low," she commanded.

Without waiting to see if he obeyed her, Holly crouched down and began working her way to the rear of the truck, keeping her weapon raised as she scanned the trees to her right, looking for any signs of movement. She blinked hard, peering through the thick smoke, and forced herself to move forward one step at a time. Her hands were slick on the assault rifle she carried and for a moment the only thing she heard was her own breathing, rapid and shallow. She forced herself to take several deep breaths and concentrated firmly on her goal.

If she and the sergeant could reach the other trucks, she knew they would be safe. Behind her, another explosion rent the air and the force of the blast threw her forward onto the ground. Martinez plowed into her back, and for a moment the two of them lay sprawled in the dirt, stunned.

Sgt. Martinez recovered first, rolling to his knees and

dragging Holly upward. "Move, damn it!" he shouted. "Move!"

Glancing over her shoulder, Holly saw it was the engine compartment of their own truck that had been hit. The cab where they had been sitting just moments before was fully engulfed in flames. She scrambled to her feet and made her way to the next truck, and then the next, until a movement from the trees to her right made her stop and swing her weapon around, ready to open fire if she needed to. Glancing back, she saw that Martinez was still two trucks behind her, crouched in a combat-ready position with his weapon raised and directed at the trees.

Refocusing her attention on where she had seen movement, she cautiously crept forward, sweeping her rifle along the tree line as she went. Whatever movement she thought she had seen was gone, and she prepared to run the short span of open space between two trucks. Then she stopped short.

"Ohmigod," she breathed.

She couldn't believe what she saw; Shane Rafferty, swinging down from the top of his gun truck, his gaze fixed grimly on her as he made a beeline directly through the line of fire toward her position. He gestured wildly back toward her truck, but Holly couldn't tell if he wanted her to be aware of the fire and move away from it, or run back toward it. She shook her head, not understanding.

Through the haze, Holly could see his eyes blazing at her. He yelled something to her and gestured again, but his words were lost beneath the sound of explosives. Holly stayed glued to where she stood, unable to tell where the precise threat came from amidst so much

chaos. Shane held his own weapon low and strafed the
orchard with gunfire as he ran. And just when Holly
thought he might actually make it across the open space
to her side, it happened.

The bullet hit him in the left leg, just below his knee.
Shane staggered, his face expressing surprise. He managed to take three more steps before his leg buckled
and he went down. Even then, he didn't stop but began
doggedly working his way across the ground toward
her.

Holly found herself running toward him before she
was aware that her feet were moving. Shane was no longer watching her, but was staring at something behind
her, his expression one of dismay. He shouted something unintelligible, and Holly felt a hard slap against
her shoulder, spinning her sideways and causing her
to stumble. She scarcely had time to register what had
happened, when an explosion rocked the ground, lifting
her off her feet and sending her sprawling onto her back.
For an instant, she couldn't breathe. Couldn't move.

Couldn't comprehend that the unthinkable had
happened.

Had it been a grenade, or a IED? Slowly, she lifted
her head and made a mental inventory of her injuries.
Her back ached, and the exposed skin of her face and
neck had been sandblasted by the dirt that had been
flung up from the explosion. Her ears were ringing and
the ground seemed to tilt beneath her. From the convoy,
she saw another soldier had taken control of Shane's gun
and was spraying the orchard with a constant barrage
of fire. Through the swirling dust and settling debris,
she could just make out Shane's prone body lying on
the ground.

Holly became aware of a fierce burning sensation in her arm and glanced down, noting the darkening stain on the camouflage of her sleeve. Her left arm hung at an awkward angle and when she probed the area, raw pain sliced through her. Her hand came away covered with blood. She'd been hit, and from the total weakness in her arm, she knew the bone was broken. Cradling the injured arm against her side, she pushed herself to her feet and staggered over to Shane. He lay face down in the dirt and even when she saw the trickle of dark blood seeping into the ground beneath him, she refused to believe he might be dead.

"Please, God," she breathed. *Just let him live and I promise I won't ask for anything more. Just let him live. Let him live.*

Holly had heard about the effects of adrenaline giving people unnatural and amazing strength during high-stress situations, but she'd never experienced it until that moment. Reaching down, she hauled on the straps of Shane's vest with her good hand and dragged him toward the trucks, digging her heels in and managing to move him across thirty feet of open ground with seemingly little effort.

Only when she had reached the safety of the trucks did two soldiers and a medic come forward to help her, lifting Shane's body and carrying him to the rear of the convoy. With Shane out of harm's way, Holly realized she was panting and light-headed and soaked with sweat. A fourth soldier caught her as she staggered, and supported her weight as he hustled her to a secure spot behind a truck and lowered her to a sitting position against one of its enormous tires.

She strained for a glimpse of Shane, stretched out on

the dirt road as the medics worked on him. Around her, the sounds of battle continued. The world spun dizzyingly and Holly dropped her head to her knees, dragging in great gulps of air. Fear consumed her, so intense that she was certain her heart would stop beating. Her stomach twisted in a sickening knot. She didn't know what she would do if Shane died. The very thought made her go weak. Blackness fluttered at the edge of her vision, and she was only vaguely aware of sliding sideways onto the ground…and then she knew nothing more.

SHE WAS HAVING the dream again, but this time it seemed so *real*…she could actually feel Shane's hands on her, unbuttoning her shirt and exposing her skin to the cool air. His fingers brushed over her flesh, causing a thrill of awareness to shoot through her. She moaned softly and arched upward, seeking more of the delicious contact. She'd wanted this for so many years and now here he was, touching her, and even if it was only a dream, Holly didn't want to miss a second of it.

The faint odor of gasoline hung on the air, and overhead she could hear the soft whir of a ceiling fan; they were in the boathouse, where Shane preferred to sleep whenever he came to stay at her family's summer place. How many times had she been tempted to follow him here? To undress and spread herself across the bed in the small bunk room and show him how good it could be between them? She wasn't a kid anymore, and it was time he stopped thinking of her as his best friend's little sister. She'd caught him watching her when he thought she wasn't looking, and the expression in his hazel eyes told her that he wanted her, too. Only his damnable honor and pride kept him from accepting everything she had to offer.

But not now.

For this moment, at least, he was hers, and even if this was just a dream, she'd take it. As dreams went, it was a pretty good one. Her entire body was on fire with need.

"Shane," she breathed, "kiss me."

"Holly." His voice sounded strained, with an underlying urgency that she had never heard before. He didn't sound at all like the Shane she knew. "Holly, stay with me."

She frowned. Stay with him? Of course she intended to stay with him. She'd opted for an assignment in Iraq because that's where he was stationed. Practically every decision she'd made over the past seven years had been for one reason: Shane Rafferty. Oh yeah, she intended to stay with him.

His touch was incredibly gentle as he eased the fabric of her blouse back, and Holly shifted to grant him better access. As she did so, agonizing pain flared in her shoulder and made her cry out, jerking her out of the sensual dream and into a harsh reality that was equally as surreal.

Through a haze of pain, Holly opened her eyes and saw two soldiers crouched over her. One of them cut away the sleeve of her camo jacket with a knife while the second one prepared an I.V. drip. She concentrated on the face of the first man and struggled to bring him into focus. Not Shane.

Slowly, she became aware that they were in a military helicopter, and Holly could smell fumes from the aviation fuel. What she'd dreamed was the soft whir of a ceiling fan was, in reality, the rhythmic thwap-thwap of the rotor blades. All around her, male voices barked orders while others were raised in urgent discussion. None of those voices belonged to Shane.

"Stay with me, Lieutenant," the first soldier commanded, his eyes flicking to hers. "You're going to be fine."

Her entire body ached, but her left arm burned with an intensity that made it difficult to breathe. Holly shifted her gaze to where the soldier probed at her shoulder. There was so much blood soaking her clothing and covering his hands that at first, she couldn't tell where it came from. Then, as he pulled away a bloodied gauze pad, she saw the gaping wound high on her upper arm. She had a hole the size of a half-dollar and bone fragments protruded through ragged flesh around it. Blood pumped in a slow, steady flow from the injury even as the medic tried to staunch it. Immediately, her head felt woozy and a wave of nausea washed over her. She turned her face away and struggled to draw in air.

"What happened?" Her voice was little more than a hoarse whisper.

"Your supply convoy drove into an ambush," the first soldier said curtly. "You were shot, but you're going to be fine."

She'd been shot?

She struggled to remember, and images drifted through her mind, as hazy and insubstantial as smoke. Sifting through them, she winced as she recalled the attack.

As she turned her face away from where the medic was working on her arm, she realized there was an injured soldier on a gurney next to her, and two medics were frantically working over his prone body. The medics blocked her view of his face, but she recognized the black tribal tattoo that encircled his bicep.

Shane.

Holly tried to raise herself on her good elbow to get a better look at him. They had stripped him of his protective body armor and camo jacket and...oh, God, there was so much blood covering his muscled torso. The medics bent over him, while another barked into a radio. All she heard was "men down, one urgent." She knew what urgent meant—loss of life was imminent without immediate medical intervention, and not the kind that they could provide on the battlefield.

Shane was going to die.

Another wave of dizziness swept over her.

"Shane." Her voice was no more than a gasp.

"Lieutenant, I'm going to sedate you," said the medic who crouched over her. He pushed her back down and the second soldier deftly inserted an intravenous drip into her uninjured arm. Almost instantly, the agonizing pain in her shoulder subsided and Holly had the oddest sensation that she was floating.

She could see Shane's face now, it was covered in dust and blood, but there was no mistaking the strong line of his jaw, the proud nose and thrusting cheekbones, the dark shadow of his lashes against his cheeks. A thin trickle of blood ran from his ear and nose. The sight made Holly feel light-headed, or maybe that was the effect of the morphine they had given her. She could no longer tell.

Closing her eyes, she drifted in a strange euphoria. The sounds of the helicopter and the men's voices faded to a distant hum. She was back in the boathouse, and

Shane was there with her. He smiled down at her and she raised her arms to welcome him into her embrace, stroking her hands over the hot silk of his skin and knowing this would be the last time they would ever be together. In the morning, he would be gone. She determinedly pushed aside the sadness that filled her. They were together now, and that was all that mattered.

With a soft sigh, she melted into his arms.

2

THE LAST PERSON SHANE Rafferty expected to see walk through the door of his hospital room was his father. A pang of guilt swept through him. He'd been back in the States for nearly a month while the staff at the U.S. Naval Hospital patched him up, yet he hadn't talked to his old man. The nurses had told him that his father had kept a near constant vigil at his bedside for the first two weeks that he'd been in the hospital, when Shane had lain in a drug-induced coma. But once he'd turned the corner to recovery, his father had returned to his home in Chatham. He'd left messages on Shane's cell phone, but Shane hadn't returned any of his calls. He told himself it was because his father was a busy man and he hadn't wanted to worry him, but he knew that was a lie.

He hadn't wanted to see him.

James Rafferty looked older than Shane remembered. His dark hair was liberally streaked with gray and his strong face was lined with deep seams. His expression was wary as he approached Shane's bed, as if he wasn't sure he'd be welcome.

"Hello, son."

His father's dark eyes swept once over Shane's body, his gaze touching briefly on the fading cuts and bruises that marred Shane's face, neck, and arms, before lingering on the cast that enveloped his left leg from the knee down to his toes. His father's throat worked convulsively, but when he met Shane's eyes, he schooled his expression.

"How you feeling, boy?"

Like shit, he wanted to respond. It had been nearly four weeks since the incident, and yet Shane's entire body still ached, and his skin felt as if it had been sandblasted. His newly healed wounds felt pinched and tight. He had a bitch of a headache, and if he didn't know better, he'd have thought he'd taken a direct hit from a rocket launched missile. But according to reports, it had been a hand grenade, and he'd been lucky—he'd been on the outer edge of the impact radius and might have sustained more serious injuries, but the bullet that had taken him out at the knees had also saved his life. If he hadn't already been on the ground, he likely would have been killed.

So how was he doing? He shrugged. "I'm okay."

The doctors had stitched him up and repaired his fractured leg and told him not to worry, he'd make a full recovery. But what they hadn't warned him about were the nightmares that dragged him out of sleep each night, his heart racing and his body coated in sweat. They were always the same; he was sprinting through the battle towards Holly. He could see her standing there, staring at him in horror through the smoke and debris, and he was driven by a desperate need to reach her. But he never made it. Each time, he'd watch her die before he could save her. Each time, her death was an agony that tore him apart. Then he'd wake up and realize he'd only been dreaming, but it would be long minutes before his heart rate slowed and his breathing returned to normal. He'd lie in bed and remind himself that Holly was alive, until the words became his mantra. *She's alive. She's alive. She's alive.*

He didn't know what he would do if anything happened to her. He'd spent the better part of the last ten years fighting his powerful attraction to her and telling himself that they had no future together, when the truth was he couldn't envision a future—any future—without her in it. He might not be the right guy for her, but he wouldn't hesitate to lay down his life to save hers. She was the reason he'd joined the military in the first place. One, he'd needed to get out of Chatham and away from Holly before he did something completely stupid, like sleep with her. Two, she came from a military family and he knew how much she respected service men and women. Part of him had dared to hope that if he joined the military *and* if he worked hard to rise through the ranks and if he could distinguish himself somehow, then maybe—just maybe—he could be worthy of her.

But then the unthinkable had happened; Holly had also joined the military and had somehow managed to end up assigned to the same base as himself. He wasn't naive enough to believe any of it was coincidence, but he had a difficult time figuring out what it was she saw in him that would make her request a deployment to Iraq when she could have had her choice of assignments. Since the day she arrived at Al Asad Air Base, his mission had abruptly switched from combat to keeping her safe.

But he couldn't escape the fact that his recurring

nightmares had almost become reality. Holly had very nearly been killed. He'd read the incident report a dozen times, but the damned thing was he couldn't recall a single detail of that day, or the attack that had nearly ended his life. The doctors told him the amnesia was temporary; a direct result of the concussion he'd sustained from the grenade. He'd been assured that his memory would return, but Shane had a nagging sense of unease that until it did, he was missing something vital.

"I wanted to come back sooner, but we've been busy at the track, what with the Preakness coming up next month," his father was saying. He shifted uncomfortably. "But I'd have come anyway, if you'd wanted me to."

Which clearly Shane hadn't or he would have called him. His father didn't say the words, but it was all there on his face.

Shane sighed.

"You didn't need to come all the way up here," he finally said, referring to the four-hour drive from Chatham, Virginia, to the medical center in Washington, D.C. "They're releasing me today."

James Rafferty dragged a hand through his hair and a fleeting frown crossed his face. "But that's why I came," he finally said. "To bring you home."

Home.

Images of the three-room apartment over Benjamin's Drugstore flitted through Shane's mind. That cramped space had never been home to Shane. He hadn't had a home since the day his mother had died and he and his father had moved to the pristine community of Chatham. The place may as well have been called Stepford, with its immaculate, white-pillared mansions and perfect, tree-lined streets. He'd fit into the quaint town like a rough-hewn square peg into a neat, round hole.

After the death of his mother, Shane's father had withdrawn from everyone, including Shane. For nearly two years, he did little except drink and sleep. First he'd lost his job, and then he'd lost the house until, eventually, the only thing his father had left was his reputation—and Shane had known that unless they acted quickly, he'd lose that, too. His father had needed another job and the only thing he really knew was horses. Race horses, to be precise. He'd trained some of the best horses ever to run a racetrack, and once Shane had put the word out that his father was ready to get back into the business, the offers had begun trickling in.

Shane had chosen a job for his father at a stable in Chatham, despite the fact the position was not lead trainer. After two years away from the track, his father had needed to prove himself before anyone would give him that kind of opportunity again. It had taken several years, but James Rafferty was firmly back on his feet and despite the fact he could afford a new home, he hadn't left the tiny apartment over the drug store, insisting that it suited his needs.

But returning to Chatham was the last thing Shane wanted to do, not because of his father but because of *her*. She'd be at her parents' home, recovering from her own injuries and Shane didn't want to risk running into her. Too much had happened for them to ever go back to the way things had been when they were teenagers.

He'd first seen Holly Durant soon after he'd moved to Chatham. He'd been barely seventeen and he'd taken a job working at the drugstore. Holly and her clique of giggling, sashaying girlfriends from Chatham Hall, the affluent girls' boarding school in town where she was a day student, had liked to come into the drugstore for after school. He still probably never would have met her if he hadn't become friends with her older brother, Mitch. Even then, when he and Mitch had become damn near inseparable and Shane spent more time at the Durant house than he did at his own, he hadn't really made an effort to get to know Holly. He didn't want to know her. Just the thought of talking to her had terrified him.

She'd been too pretty. Too mouthy.

Too good for him.

So he'd all but ignored her, telling himself there was no sense in chasing a pipe dream. Look where it had gotten his father. Nope, better to stick with what you knew and stay where you belonged.

And he definitely didn't belong in Chatham.

He couldn't imagine he'd be welcome there now, anyway, not after what had happened. Holly's father was a retired Navy admiral and he and Holly's mother were keystones of the small community. Shane had nothing but admiration and respect for them and he didn't think he could bear their censure. After all, he'd let them down.

He'd let *her* down. He'd failed her.

He should have protected Holly but instead, he'd nearly gotten her killed. He'd read the incident report, which indicated he'd abandoned his position atop the gun truck and had raced through the firefight toward Holly *without due cause*. He might not be able to recall the attack, but he could guess why he'd done it—he'd wanted to protect Holly. Instead, she'd been forced to protect him and had nearly been killed in the process.

"I'm not going home," he said darkly.

His father's eyebrows drew together. "What do you mean you're not coming home? I ain't touched your room. It's just the same as when you left it." He indicated Shane's leg. "'Course, the stairs might give you some trouble, but we'll manage."

"I said I'm not going back."

"Where will you go, then? You got no place else to stay." His father sounded baffled.

Shane looked away. He was right. He had nowhere else to go. He'd joined the military in order to get away from his father, from Holly, and from Chatham. Since then, he'd never stayed in one place long enough to buy a house or even lease an apartment. The doctors said he couldn't return to active duty for at least three weeks, maybe longer. He could probably stay at the Marine barracks in Washington, D.C. or the Marine Corps base in Quantico until he recuperated, but the prospect held little appeal for him.

"He's going to stay at the lake house."

Both men turned at the sound of the deep voice, but Shane's father was the first to recover, striding forward to grasp Mitch Durant's hand and pump it furiously.

"Hell, boy," he said, "it's damned nice to see you. How long has it been? Three years? Four? You look good. The uniform suits you. How's your sister? I hear she saved my boy's life. I'd like to thank her properly, if she's up for a visit."

In his crisp Navy dress uniform, Mitch looked every inch an officer and a gentleman. The double silver bars on his collar denoted his rank as Lieutenant and for the first time, Shane was acutely conscious of the difference in their status. The last he'd heard, Mitch was doing a

six-month deployment aboard the USS Lincoln, an air-
craft carrier that patrolled Middle Eastern waters. He'd
obviously come home to be with his sister and another
pang of guilt washed over Shane.

"Holly will recover, sir," Mitch was saying. "Her arm
is busted up pretty good, but otherwise she's okay."

He was glossing over her condition, and Shane knew
it. By the time he'd regained consciousness and recovered enough to even think about Holly, he'd been told
that she'd already been released from the hospital. He'd
persisted in knowing her condition and after days of
badgering the nursing staff he'd learned that the bone
in her arm had been shattered by the bullet, and only a
series of metal plates and screws had been able to repair
it.

And it was all his fault. If he'd just stayed with his
gun, instead of trying to be a hero...

Mitch walked toward Shane's bed with careful deliberation. He extended his hand and Shane took it.

"Hey, man," Mitch said. "How're you doing?"

"I'm okay."

To his immense relief, there was no censure in Mitch's
eyes, no recriminations. Only the same genuine warmth
and friendship that he had grown to rely on since they
were kids.

"You look like hell," Mitch observed, one corner of
his mouth lifting in a wry grin. "But I think it might
actually be an improvement."

Shane knew he referred to the lacerations and bruises
on his face. He had seen his reflection for the first time
that morning, when the nurses had finally relented and
let him take a real shower on his own. They'd seemed
disappointed when he'd declined the bedside sponge

baths they had been providing him each day since his arrival. To his way of thinking, their dedication to his hygiene had been just a tad too thorough.

Shane felt a reluctant smile tug at his mouth. "Yeah, well you always were jealous of my good looks." He glanced over at his father and lowered his voice. "So what's this about the lake house?"

He didn't really need to ask the question. Mitch understood why he didn't want to stay with his father and by offering up the lake house, he was giving Shane an excuse not to have to. But Shane had no intention of accepting the invitation.

He couldn't think about the lake house without his imagination conjuring up images of Holly, slim and naked and sexy as hell, wrapping herself around him like she couldn't get enough of him. He'd known that she'd harbored a crush on him since she was a teenager. She'd followed him everywhere with that damned camera of hers, snapping pictures of him whenever she thought he wasn't looking. But he wasn't boyfriend material, and he definitely wasn't husband material. He'd seen what marriage to his father had done to his mother. He'd never be able to provide Holly with the kind of lifestyle she was accustomed to, and he wouldn't be responsible for turning her into a bitter, unhappy woman. Maybe if things had been different…

He could still recall that Christmas Eve, when she'd followed him down to the wine cellar and kissed him. It was the best Christmas gift he'd ever received, only he hadn't wanted to stop there. He'd wanted to consume her, to push himself into her warmth until she no longer knew where her body ended and his began.

He'd wanted to inhale her, to absorb her through his

very pores. But he'd pulled away, and he'd kept away for the next four years. He hadn't trusted himself to let her get too close. It hadn't been until the night of her graduation party that he'd let down his guard.

Holly had just graduated from the Naval Academy and her mother had sent him an invitation to help celebrate at the lake house. He was sure she'd done it more out of respect for the friendship he had with Mitch than for any relationship he had with Holly, but he hadn't been able to resist going. He'd been stationed at Camp Lejeune, so he'd requested a couple of days leave and had driven from North Carolina to the house in southwestern Virginia. He'd needed to know if his memories of her had been accurate.

They hadn't been.

Holly had been even more vibrant and beautiful than he remembered, and had a new confidence that let him know she wasn't a kid any more. She'd cut her long, dark hair into a short, sleek cap that molded her skull and made her eyes seem bigger than ever. Shane had been unable to drag his gaze from her the entire evening. He'd been stunned when she'd followed him into the boathouse late that night and began undressing in the tiny guest room, her eyes locked on his. He hadn't even tried to resist, and that one night was the closest he'd ever get to heaven.

But to go back to the lake house? No way.

As if he could read Shane's thoughts, Mitch raised an eyebrow. "Where else are you going to go? At least at the lake house, you'll have everything you need. The Jeep is there, and I can also ask Pete to check in on you every so often and bring you whatever supplies you need."

Pete Larson owned the only grocery store and gas

station on the eastern side of the lake and had known the Durant family for years. But Shane figured he could easily drive the Jeep, even with the cast on his left leg. With a sense of surprise, he realized he was actually tempted to accept Mitch's offer. More than tempted, if it meant he didn't need to go back to Chatham.

He eyed Mitch with suspicion. "What about your family? Won't they object to my staying there?"

"My folks don't get out there much anymore, but I know they wouldn't mind. Mom always liked you better than me, anyway."

Shane looked away. "What about Holly?"

Mitch's smile was wry. "She definitely liked you better than me." Seeing Shane's expression, he grew serious. "She was released from the hospital over three weeks ago. They stopped by to see you before they left, but you were still too doped up to realize it. You didn't even know they were there."

Which was just as well. Shane didn't think he could face the Durants, and if Holly had been with them... well, he *definitely* didn't want to face her. He'd never understood what she'd seen in him, but he'd rather not face her censure now. She must hate him for what had happened, if not at the lake house three years ago, then in Iraq four weeks ago.

"But she's...okay?"

Mitch snorted. "She's ready to go back to Iraq, that's how okay she is. Mother is driving her crazy, trying to anticipate her every need. She insists on treating Holly like an invalid and poor Holly is climbing the walls, probably wishing she was anywhere but home."

Shane almost smiled, he could picture it so clearly. Even as a teenager, Holly had chafed under her parents' constant supervision. Mrs. Durant was sweet and generous, but Shane knew firsthand that she could also be a little overwhelming in her attentiveness.

"So what about you?" he asked, wanting to change the subject. "How long are you home?"

Mitch shrugged. "I'm actually on my way back to my ship. I came back as soon as I heard about Holly. And you. I've been home for a couple of weeks, but I fly out tonight." He paused. "I hear you're being released. I have just enough time to drive you out to the lake, if you'd like."

"That ain't necessary." Shane's father came to stand next to Mitch. "If you won't come home with me, son, then at least let me drive you out to the lake. It's out of the Lieutenant's way, while I practically have to go by there on my way home."

Shane shook his head. "It's okay, Dad. You don't need to do that."

His father blew out a frustrated breath. "Goddammit, son, when are you going to let me do something for you? Like I said, the lake is on my way home and at least the drive would give us a chance to catch up."

Sure, Shane thought bitterly. Four hours in a car with his father, reminiscing about his crappy childhood. The combat he'd seen in Iraq had been nothing compared to the battles that had raged between his parents. He sighed in resignation.

"Sure. Fine." *Whatever.*

Mitch looked sympathetic. Shane cleared his throat. "How, um, is Holly, really?"

Mitch hesitated, as if weighing his words. "She'll be okay. She's more concerned about you than she is about herself."

Shane felt his gut twist. "I'm sorry."

"Don't be. Whatever happened out there wasn't your fault." He raked a hand over his cropped hair. "Look, I should get going. You remember where the key to the lake house is kept, right?"

"Yeah."

"If I know my mother, the pantry should be pretty well-stocked with dry goods, but call Pete Larson if you need anything," Mitch advised. "As far as the house goes, my mother has a cleaning service come in every couple of weeks to air the place out and run the water, so you should be all set."

"Thanks. I appreciate it."

"Okay, then." Mitch paused, studying the hat he held in his hands. "About Holly…I know you're probably blaming yourself, but don't."

Shane snorted. "Why not? The incident report said I abandoned my post *without due cause*. If I hadn't left my position, then I wouldn't have been shot. And if I hadn't been shot, then Holly wouldn't have put herself in danger by running out to rescue me. She would have stayed by the trucks and been safe." He gave Mitch a challenging look. "So you see, it is my fault."

Mitch looked unconvinced. "The doctors said you have a form of amnesia…that you have no recollection of what actually happened that day, so I'm sure there was a good reason why you left your gun. You're not the type of soldier who would just abandon your position."

"You don't know that."

"I know you. And I know you're not the kind of guy who gets caught up in the heat of the moment and does something stupid."

Shane glanced sharply at his friend, but Mitch's expression was sincere. He really believed what he'd just said. But what he didn't know, what Shane wasn't about to tell him, was that Holly Durant was the one person who could make him lose his head.

Again and again and again.

3

HOLLY HADN'T BEEN OUT to the lake house in years, not since she'd graduated from the Naval Academy. That night had been both the best and worst of her entire life. The best, because she'd finally known what it was like to be loved by Shane Rafferty, and the worst because... well, because she'd known that she would never experience anything like it ever again.

Now, driving along the densely wooded road that led to her parents' summer place, she wasn't prepared for how those memories made her chest ache and her throat tighten.

"Hey, you okay?"

Holly turned toward her childhood friend, Susan, and gave her a bright smile. "Yes. Absolutely. It's just that I haven't been back here in so long..."

"Mmm-hmm," her friend murmured knowingly.

Holly narrowed her eyes at her. "What is that supposed to mean?"

Susan looked away from the road long enough to give Holly a tolerant look. "I was there that night, remember?

And the next morning, after he left. I know what he did to you."

Oh no, she didn't. The things that Shane Rafferty had done to her that night still caused Holly's toes to curl in recalled pleasure.

She dragged her gaze away from Susan's and looked out the window at the passing trees. "Don't put all the blame on him. I was shameless in the way I chased after him, and it's not like he ever made any promises to me." She gave a huff of laughter. "Just the opposite, actually. He made it pretty clear that he wasn't interested in anything more than sex."

"But you were hoping…"

Yes, she had hoped. For the next three years, she'd hoped. She still hoped that his feelings ran deeper than he let on. The fact that he had abandoned his position during the fire fight to try and rescue her gave her some optimism, although knowing Shane the way she did, he probably would have done the same for anyone.

She shrugged in response to Susan's question, hoping her friend didn't see through her bravado. Let her believe that she no longer held a torch for Shane Rafferty. She'd managed to fool everyone, except herself.

"It was a one-time thing. A mistake, actually. I'm no longer interested in Shane and he's definitely not interested in me." Seeing her friend's dubious expression, she plunged on, as if by getting the words out fast enough, she might believe they were true. "Even when we were on the same base in Iraq, we didn't run into each other very much and when we did, it was just sort of awkward. We don't even have anything in common."

"So you didn't get to see him afterwards…at the hospital?"

Holly shook her head. "Not really. We went to his room before I was released, but he was still unconscious. The doctors had him in a drug-induced coma because of his head injury. They told me that even if he'd been awake, he would have been on some heavy pain meds and probably wouldn't have recognized me." She shivered in memory. "He had so many stitches where they'd removed shrapnel, and was on a breathing tube. There didn't seem much point in hanging around, and my parents were anxious to get me home."

"Poor guy. But you said he was finally released, right?"

"Yes. My father insisted on receiving a report on his progress every day. He went home a couple of days ago."

"To Chatham?" Susan sounded surprised.

"I think so. Or maybe he went back to Camp Le-Jeune." She shrugged. "I'm not sure."

"Maybe we should have stopped by the drugstore on our way out of town," mused Susan, "We could have paid him a visit. It would have been nice to have him acknowledge that you saved his life. Nothing wrong with a little groveling."

"He doesn't need to do that," Holly replied, aghast, although she did find the thought of Shane Rafferty groveling a little bit intriguing. "Besides, he was shot trying to protect me. If I hadn't insisted on driving in that convoy…"

"Listen," Susan interrupted, "you can play the blame game all you want, but the bottom line is that you're both okay. Thank God."

Holly was silent, replaying those horrific moments in Iraq when she'd believed Shane was dead. She never wanted to experience anything close to that ever again. She drew in a shuddering breath.

"Hey." Reaching over, Susan covered Holly's hand with her own. "You *are* okay, right?"

Holly nodded. "I'm fine."

She wasn't ready to confide in Susan about the phone call she'd received from the Naval hospital. Her doctor had confirmed what she had already suspected—the bullet that had shattered her upper arm had done permanent nerve damage. She might never regain full use of the limb.

The gnawing pain that had kept her awake those first two weeks had subsided to a dull ache. She'd stopped taking the pills that the doctors had prescribed because she didn't like how they made her feel woozy and disoriented. The incision where the surgeons had inserted a metal plate and screws into the upper arm bone had mostly healed, although her arm would always have a nasty scar from the bullet itself.

But what bothered her most was the annoying numbness across the back of her hand and through her fingers, and how she couldn't seem to get a good grip on anything. The doctors had run more tests, and had called her that morning with the results. The news had come as a devastating blow to Holly. Without full use of her arm, she would likely have to leave the military. Even if the top brass decided she could stay, she'd probably be placed in a desk job, overseeing administrative minutia. Her days of going on deployments were over, since she could no longer handle a weapon. In fact, she could barely handle a camera.

Her beloved camera had been lost in the explosion that had destroyed her supply truck, and her father had presented her with a brand-new one just days after she had arrived home. Holly knew the camera was the best that money could buy, but she still grieved for the one she'd lost; the one she'd had since she was a teenager. That camera had been as familiar to her as her own hand. She sighed. It seemed that nothing would ever be the same as it had been.

"So how are your parents going to react when they learn you've left?" Susan interrupted her thoughts.

Holly sighed deeply. Her parents had been playing golf with friends when Holly had made her getaway. They wouldn't be back for hours yet, but Holly didn't expect them to come after her. They would respect her need for privacy.

"They'll be hurt," she admitted. "They'll think they did something wrong. But I couldn't stay there any longer. I was…suffocating. I just needed to get out."

That was the truth. She hadn't told her parents that she was leaving, knowing they would try to dissuade her. But her mother's constant hovering had begun to wear on her nerves. Since she'd come home, Holly hadn't been permitted to do anything for herself. Her mother insisted that she spend her days relaxing in the gardens or on the enormous wrap-around porch, preferably with a cup of tea or a tall glass of lemonade. She'd drunk so much of both that it was a wonder she hadn't floated away. Her father had given her the space she needed, but his worry and concern for her had been like a palpable thing.

Holly knew her parents meant well, but she didn't think she could bear their pity when they learned her arm was permanently damaged. Her father, a retired Navy admiral, would take it the hardest. He'd been so proud the day she'd graduated from the academy and loved telling people that both of his children—his son *and* his daughter—had followed family tradition and made a career with the Navy. But Holly could just see their reaction when she told them the news; they would hover and fuss over her, trying to make things better, until she screamed with frustration. She needed this time away to come to terms with the fact that her life would likely never be the same.

Most of all, she needed to come to terms with the fact that she would never be with Shane Rafferty, not the way she'd dreamed of. The main reason she'd joined the military was to impress him, to be close to him; to follow him into battle if need be. But she'd never anticipated that she would be injured and forced to make a choice about staying in or getting out. At least in the military, she'd been able to take assignments at the same locations as him, ensuring that they moved in the same orbit. But if she was in Chatham…they would literally be worlds apart, and she had a feeling that if it were up to Shane, he'd never willingly come back.

What would she do now? All of her carefully laid plans were falling apart. Worse, she had no idea what she would do with the rest of her life. Even if she could remain with the Navy, the idea of teaching at the academy or working a desk job somewhere held little appeal for her. But if she left the military, she'd also leave her only connection to Shane. Yes, she had a lot of thinking to do.

"Here we are," Susan said quietly, and Holly looked up as the woods opened onto a large clearing. A gravel drive circled around the front of a timber frame house with a modest entry. The house was deceptive, Holly knew. Sitting on a rise overlooking the water, the back of the lake house was where the true magnificence lay. The property had belonged to the Durant family for generations, but where there had once stood a rustic cabin, the current lake house was a modern mixture of timber, stone, and glass, with an enormous wrap-around deck that boasted unobstructed views of the lake.

Holly knew that if she were to step onto the deck, she would see the lawn that swept down to the shore, where a quaint boathouse stood attached to a long dock. The small guest room over the boathouse had initially been intended as a place to change out of wet bathing suits before walking back to the main house, but a young Mitch had quickly adopted the space as his club house. When Shane had come to spend time at the lake, the boathouse had become his bunk room. If she closed her eyes, Holly could still picture him lying back against the pillows on the narrow bed, his body a mouthwatering combination of silken skin and hard muscles. And the expression in his eyes...

The memory caused a shiver of awareness to go through Holly.

Susan pulled up to the entrance and put the car into Park. "Do you want me to come in with you? Help you settle in? You said your parents haven't been out here in months. The place is probably crawling with cobwebs."

Holly smiled. "No, I'll be fine. Mum has a cleaning service come in every two weeks whether she's here, or not. They air everything out and keep the spiders down to a minimum."

"What about food? Even dry goods have a shelf life."

Holly gave her a tolerant look. "You know my mother, she keeps the house well-stocked. But I'll give Pete a call in the morning and ask him to bring out some fresh groceries, okay?" Seeing Susan's doubtful expression, Holly leaned across the center console and gave her friend a one-armed hug. "Don't worry about me. I need this time alone to get my head straight."

Susan nodded. "I know. I just hope your parents don't blame me for aiding and abetting."

Holly opened the door and climbed out, hefting her camera bag and pocketbook over her good shoulder. Leaning down to look into the car, she gave Susan what she hoped was a reassuring smile. "I'll give them a call tonight. They'll understand. Thanks for the lift."

She watched as Susan's car drove away and then she turned toward the house, fishing in her pocketbook for her set of house keys. Fitting the key into the front door, she was dismayed to find it already unlocked. Had the housecleaners forgotten to lock up after they left? Holly stood for a moment, undecided. She had her cell phone with her, but if there was an intruder in the house, it could take up to twenty minutes for the police to make their way out to the lake.

Gathering up her courage, Holly pushed the door open and entered, looking cautiously around for anything out of place, but the house was quiet. She closed the door and set her camera bag and pocketbook on the floor, and then made her way up the stairs to the main living area. As always, the soaring timber ceilings and wall of windows overlooking the water took her breath away. Almost without realizing it, she walked toward the glass. Being at the lake house brought her a sense of calm that she hadn't felt in months. Years, even. She could almost feel the stress start to fall away.

In the next instant, Holly gave a startled gasp and nearly fell over in her haste to step back from the windows. A half-naked man lay on a chaise on the massive wrap-around deck, under the cover of an enormous umbrella. With her heart still stuttering in her chest, she peered through the glass. His lounge chair faced the lake and she couldn't see his face, but what she could see caused her entire body to go tense.

Shane Rafferty.

Even without seeing his features, she recognized those broad shoulders and the black tribal tattoo that encircled one bicep. He wore a pair of dark shorts, with his legs stretched out in front of him. His left leg was encased in an olive colored cast from his knee to his toes, and Holly's chest tightened.

Her head swirled with thoughts. What was he doing out here? Had he guessed she'd be at the lake house, too? If not, how would he react when he saw her? What should she do? How should she act? He was the last person she'd ever expected to see. She knew him well enough to know that he would never come out to the lake without an invitation, but her parents hadn't mentioned that he was staying here. Which meant her brother, Mitch, had likely extended the invite. Holly moved on trembling legs away from the windows, her heart thudding hard against her ribs as her mind worked furiously.

She should leave.

But she desperately wanted to stay.

He wouldn't be happy to see her. He'd insist on leaving at the first opportunity. He'd probably call Pete and ask him to come out immediately and drive him back into town.

Holly hadn't had a chance to talk with Shane following the incident, and her enduring memory was of him lying bloodied and unresponsive on the gurney beside her while the medics worked frantically over him. Seeing him now, whole and safe, made her feel a little boneless with relief. Every cell in her body urged her to go outside and show him how she felt; to wrap herself around him and draw him inside herself.

Blowing out a hard breath, Holly mounted the stairs to the bedrooms. Shane would never let himself lose control with her again, the way he had that night in the boathouse. He'd all but said as much to her when she'd arrived at Al Asad Air Base in Iraq.

First and foremost was the fact that she outranked him. Any fraternization between them could result in a court-martial and dishonorable discharge for either of them. Shane might not have been born into a military family, like she had been, but he was more of a soldier than she would ever be. Holly believed that if he were booted out of the military, he might never forgive himself—or her—for letting it happen.

She also knew from experience that if she followed through on her instincts, Shane wouldn't be able to resist her, but any relationship with him would only be physical. He'd made that completely clear. He was totally committed to the Marine Corps and there was no way he'd make any promises to her, no matter how unbelievably great the sex was.

And it had been great.

Off the charts great.

And while Holly lived in hopeful anticipation of a

repeat performance, the strong pull of attraction she felt was just one aspect of his overall appeal. She wanted— no, *needed*—more. She needed to be part of his world. To be connected to him, and acknowledged by him. To know that she mattered.

Pushing her hand through her short hair, she walked over to her bedroom window and carefully turned the slatted wood blinds so that she could peek down at the deck. The angle was all wrong, though, and the umbrella completely obscured the lounge chair and its occupant. Holly let out a shuddering breath and closed the blinds.

Shane was *here*. Alive. Whole.

She moved blindly toward the bed and sank down, considering the implications of being here with him. Alone.

Nobody knew they were together, and even if her parents talked with Mitch and figured it out, the information would never go outside the family. There was no risk of anyone in their military chain of command finding out, not that she and Shane had anything to hide. After all, it wasn't as if they were actually sleeping together.

But given the chance, Holly knew she would. She'd take Shane Rafferty any way she could get him. That day on the battlefield, when she'd been so certain he would die, she'd made a promise that if he survived, she would never ask for anything else.

She'd lied.

She knew now that she'd been given a second chance. She'd been crazy about Shane for as long as she could remember, but with the exception of that one night, she'd allowed Shane to determine the tenor of their relationship and permitted him to maintain both a physical and emotional distance between them.

But now here they were.

Holly drew in a deep breath, knowing what she had to do. She needed to change the rules. After all, what did she have to lose? Eventually, Shane would return to active duty and she wouldn't. Losing him was inevitable. But for now, he was here. She would take a chance and grab whatever she could, and pray that when the time came to let him go, it would be enough.

With a new sense of purpose, Holly stripped out of her jeans and shirt, taking care not to strain her arm, and began rummaging through her dresser for a swimsuit. She wouldn't come on too strong, initially. His first instinct would be to leave, so she'd play it cool and let him get accustomed to the idea of sharing the lake house with her. She'd gotten past his defenses once; she could do it again.

Pulling out a tiny blue bikini, she frowned and discarded it as too provocative. She knew Shane well enough to know that seeing her in the flimsy scraps of cloth would make him acutely aware of her, but he'd probably glower and tell her to cover up. But she had a modest one-piece suit that nobody could call alluring. Pulling it out, she tossed it onto the bed and was in the process of unfastening the front clasp of her bra when she heard a sound at her bedroom door, something between a groan and a sigh.

Whirling around, she stilled, and every good intention she had went flying out the window. Shane stood frozen in her doorway, leaning heavily on a cane, and the expression in his eyes caused tiny flickers of heat to rise up on her skin. His gaze devoured her, traveling downward to linger on her breasts, where her fingers paused over the clasp of the bra, and then lower, to her hips and thighs. When he met her eyes again, they were hot with hunger.

"Holly," he finally said in a strangled voice. "What are you doing here?"

"Shane." Her blood began a slow, languorous churning through her veins. "I—I was just coming downstairs to say hello. I needed to get away, to be alone. That is— not completely alone, just away from my parents. You don't need to leave—I mean, I don't mind you staying. You should stay. I want you to stay."

God, she was babbling like an idiot, but was it any surprise? The way he looked, combined with the expression in his eyes, made it difficult for her to think straight. Wearing nothing but a pair of shorts low on his hips, he was all thrusting shoulders and muscle-banded abdomen. But where Holly remembered acres of smooth, tanned skin, Shane's torso was now marred with a dozen or more scars, still vivid and raw, and the faded smudging of bruises.

Emotion swelled in her chest. She swallowed hard and schooled her features, unwilling to let him see how his injuries affected her. A strip of pale flesh rode just above his waistband, and her fingers itched to explore the narrow strip of dark hair that began just beneath his navel and disappeared beneath the fabric of his shorts. The room seemed suddenly too small and too warm.

He took a step into the room, his eyes fastened on her. He gave no indication that he'd even heard her. His breathing was uneven, and every muscle in his body seemed tightly coiled. "How are you?" His voice was hoarse. "I mean, are you okay?"

She struggled to think coherently, when all she wanted to do was launch herself into his arms. She swallowed hard. "I'm fine. What about you? I've thought about you so much."

"God, Holly."

His anguished voice seemed to reach into her most secret places. Her heart began to thump hard, until she could feel her blood vibrating in her temples, in her fingertips, throughout her body, until the throbbing sensation finally centered in the warm, damp place between her thighs.

In the next instant she was in his arms, her hands clutching his broad shoulders as he hugged her tightly against his chest. Holly buried her face against his neck and breathed in his scent, relishing the feel of his strong hands against her back.

"Oh, Shane," she breathed, and drew back just enough to look into his eyes.

"I'm sorry," he groaned, in the instant before he lowered his head and claimed her mouth with his.

HOLLY'S MOUTH WAS SOFT and lush and hot, exactly the way he remembered. Her body was slim and supple and his hands slid downward to cup her bottom and press her hips against where he was already hard for her.

She was here. Warm and alive and in his arms, kissing him back with a fierceness that caused every cell in his body to stand at attention. Even now, with her tongue in his mouth and her sweet ass cradled in his palms, he could scarcely believe she was real. How many times had he fantasized about this very thing? He knew he should push her away; set her aside and put some distance between them, but he was incapable of breaking the delicious contact.

Every fantasy he'd ever had of Holly Durant—and he'd had more than his share—was playing out in front of him, and he wasn't about to do anything to ruin it. His brain had blinked off the instant he'd caught sight of her wearing a pair of miniscule panties and a bra that did nothing to conceal the most insanely perfect pair of breasts he had ever seen. And now she was kissing him as if her very life depended on it.

He should be used to her sensual attacks; she'd stalked him from the time she was fifteen years old, but he found his ability to resist her had evaporated beneath the silken heat of her mouth on his and her hands on his skin.

He couldn't breathe. Couldn't think straight.

Desire slammed into him, fierce and hard, and his blood hummed in his veins. Sweet Christ, she was the most gorgeous woman he had ever seen. She tasted like sweet berries, and her fragrance teased his senses, and only the zipper on his shorts kept his rampant hard-on from surging forward.

The microscopic part of his brain that still functioned was firing warning shots across his bow. He was all wrong for her. He could never give her what she needed. He didn't deserve her. Even if she didn't have the good sense to realize it, he did. He dragged his mouth from hers and sucked in air.

"Holly," he finally managed, his voice sounding strained and thick, even to his own ears. "We can't do this."

But she only pressed closer, her eyes soft and hazy as she gazed up at him. "Yes, we can," she contradicted him softly, and she pressed a moist kiss against the skin beneath his collarbone. Sensation shuddered through him.

To hell with doing what was right. Nothing could prevent him from reaching for Holly, not even the sound of his cane as it clattered, unheeded, onto the floor. The warning shots had come too late; he'd just taken a direct hit and he was going down.

4

HOLLY GASPED SOFTLY as Shane bent his head and his lips covered hers, but he didn't just kiss her; he *consumed* her. His mouth plundered hers, hot and sweet, and she welcomed the erotic slide of his tongue against her own. He shifted so that his hard thigh intruded between hers, and Holly gave a soft moan of need as she felt the unmistakable thrust of his arousal. Immediately, he pulled back, his hands jerking away from her body.

"What? Did I hurt you? Jesus, I almost forgot about your arm—"

"No, my arm is fine," she assured him breathlessly, reaching for him. "Please don't stop." Grasping his hand, she drew it back to cover her breast. Beneath his fingers, her nipple tightened, jutting against his callused palm. "Now kiss me again."

This time, Shane drew her into his arms with a gentleness that was almost reverent. But his kiss was no less heated as he explored her mouth with a slow thoroughness that caused a sharp stab of arousal low in her abdomen. One hand moved to the front clasp of her bra, and with a quick flick the garment fell open. He cupped her breast and teased her nipple, rolling it between his fingers. Holly shuddered lightly when he dragged his mouth along the line of her neck and lower, to the soft skin of her breast, before drawing the distended tip into his mouth. The slippery hot sensation of his tongue flicking against her sensitized flesh was almost more than she could stand, and she moaned again, arching against him. This time, Shane didn't pull away. Slipping one hand beneath her panties, he curved his fingers over her bottom and stroked her pliant flesh.

"Jesus, you're so soft," he murmured against her lips. "I've never forgotten how goddamned soft your skin is."

He'd never forgotten.

Any misgivings Holly had vanished as she melted against him with a sigh. "I want you to touch me," she breathed. "Everywhere."

Shane groaned and took her mouth again, spearing his tongue against hers as his hands roamed over her back, his fingers tracing the curves and dips of her spine. He turned her up against the wall, pinning her there with the weight of his body. Slowly, he eased the straps of her bra down her arms until it slid free. His mouth was fused to hers and his hands explored her freely, cupping and caressing her breasts before splaying across her back and downward, to tease the soft crease of her buttocks. Holly felt a little stunned by his actions and light-headed with pleasure.

"Damn," he breathed against her lips. "I want to sweep you up and carry you over to that bed. But I can't."

In answer, Holly stepped out of his arms but didn't release his hands. Not wanting to do anything that might ruin the moment and make him have any second thoughts, she drew him toward the bed.

"I don't need to be carried," she assured him. "I just need you to join me." When she reached the mattress, she sat down and then reclined back on the coverlet, her fingers still entwined with Shane's. He didn't require any further encouragement, but came over her like a big, sleek cat, bracing his hands on either side of her as he bent to kiss her once more.

Holly tunneled her fingers through his short hair, reveling in the velvety-rough texture. He smelled good, like coconut suntan lotion. He slanted his mouth across her lips for better access, mating his tongue with hers until Holly shifted restlessly beneath him, wanting more. She gave a squeak of surprise and clutched at him with her good arm when he eased one hand beneath her and hefted her more fully onto the mattress.

"Much better," he said against her mouth, as he lowered himself alongside her, bracing his weight on one elbow and using his free hand to leisurely stroke and explore her body. He covered one breast, his long fingers kneading the firm flesh before plucking at the nipple. The combination of his tongue in her mouth and his hand on her breast sent a rush of heat and moisture to her core, and she arched helplessly against him.

There hadn't been anyone serious in her life since the night she'd spent with him at the lake house. No one made her feel the way he did; hot and achy and trembling with need. And she knew instinctively that no man could bring her the pleasure that Shane did. From the start, it seemed he knew just how to touch her so that she felt crazed with lust.

"Oh, man," Shane rasped, pulling back slightly, "you are so incredibly sexy."

Holly's breath was coming in short pants, and the expression in his eyes as he followed the path of his hand across her skin made her feel wanton. Her center throbbed, and she knew if he touched her there, she would be slick and hot. As if he could read her thoughts, he smoothed his hand across her stomach and then hooked his thumbs in the waistband of her panties and slid them down her legs. He sifted his fingers through the springy curls at the juncture of thighs. Her legs were pressed together, but all it took was a simple nudge of his hand for them to fall open.

Holly's breath hissed in when Shane bent his head to suckle her breast at the same instant he cupped her intimately, holding her in the warm palm of his hand. But it wasn't enough, and Holly shifted restlessly to gain more of the delicious contact.

"Is this what you want?" he murmured against her skin, just before he parted her slick folds with his fingers.

Holly made a strangled sound of pleasure and threaded her fingers through his scalp, holding his head to her breast. Pleasure lashed through her as he drew his fingers over her moisture, teasing but never touching the small rise of flesh that throbbed for his touch. If she'd had a little more courage, she might have dragged his hand to where she needed it the most, but she found herself embarrassed by the strength of her own arousal.

"Oh, yeah," Shane breathed, "this is definitely what you want." Holly's breath hissed inward and her hips bucked as he finally stroked her clit and then eased a finger inside her.

"Oh, God," she moaned, shocked at how needy her voice sounded and how greedily her flesh clutched at him. She'd fantasized about this for so long and part of her had wondered if her memories of their one night together had been colored by the alcohol they'd both consumed. Maybe they hadn't been as great together as she remembered. Maybe she'd built it up in her mind into something it wasn't.

But now, with Shane's body pressed against hers, and his voice murmuring husky words of encouragement in her ear, she knew her memory hadn't failed her. If anything, this experience was even more intense than their first encounter. This time, there was no darkness to conceal them, and no question that they both knew exactly what they were doing.

"Tell me what you want," he urged, and thrust his finger deeper. "Say the words."

"You know what I want." *What she'd always wanted. Him.*

Her voice sounded strained and hoarse. She raised her hips, lifting herself into the pleasure he provided.

"Tell me anyway." His voice was low and commanding, and so sexy that Holly couldn't refuse. "I want to hear it."

"I want you."

He made a sound of satisfaction deep in his throat and quickened the movements of his hand. "How do you want me?"

Any way I can get you. "Inside me. Now."

In answer, Shane withdrew from her and stood up, balancing awkwardly on his good leg as he made quick work of his shorts. Holly was glad she was already lying down, because the sight of a naked, rampantly aroused

Shane caused her legs to feel a little wobbly and her mouth to go dry. She hadn't gotten a good look at him during their previous encounter in the boathouse, and although she'd known he was impressive, she hadn't realized just how gorgeous he was. Everywhere.

He didn't give her time to admire him, however. Instead, he caught her knees in his hands and bent her legs backwards, exposing her to his gaze. Holly should have felt embarrassed, but she was way past that point. Holding her legs wide, he stepped between them. His face was taut with desire, his gaze fixed on her.

"Wait!" she exclaimed, reaching down to cover herself with one hand and prevent him from making any contact with her. "I don't have any protection, do you?"

If she weren't feeling so desperate, Holly might have laughed at the expression of dismay on his face.

"No. I didn't exactly plan—" he began, frustrated.

"It's okay," she said. "If I know my brother, he keeps a stash in his room."

"Second drawer of the dresser, in the back," Shane confirmed with a crooked smile, releasing Holly's legs. "At least, that's where he used to hide them."

"It'll be quicker if I go," she said, and without giving him a chance to argue, she bounced off the bed and shot him a seductive smile. "Don't start without me."

SHANE SAT DOWN on the bed and raked a hand over his hair. What the hell was he doing? He should stand up and walk out of the room and not look back. He shouldn't even think of screwing around with Holly Durant—but holy God, he'd never seen anything as amazing as Holly bounding back into the room, triumphantly holding four condoms in one hand, her breasts bouncing gently and the long muscles in her taut thighs flexing. Any thoughts of retreat vanished.

"We're in luck." She grinned, and pushed him down onto the mattress. Before Shane realized her intent, she straddled his hips. "There's a whole box of them, although God knows how long they've been there. Let's hope they haven't expired."

Even if they had, Shane realized he'd take the risk. He wanted Holly more than he'd ever wanted anything in his life.

Reaching up, he covered her breasts with his hands, enjoying the weight of them in his palms. She sighed and rocked her hips against his, rubbing herself along his shaft until he had to grit his teeth against the exquisite sensation. But when she reached down and took him in her hand, he groaned out loud. The sight of her slender fingers wrapped around his swollen flesh was incredibly erotic. He let her stroke him for several long seconds, until she slid her thumb across the crest where it glistened with moisture.

"Easy," he grunted. "I'm not going to last if you keep that up."

He took the condoms from her, tossing the extras aside and tearing one free from the wrapper. Holding his cock in one hand, he sheathed himself with fingers that visibly trembled. Glancing at Holly's face, he saw her eyes were fixed on him and her face looked flushed. Her nipples thrust outward, and she continued to rock softly against him.

With his hands on her waist, Shane urged her up and fitted himself against her opening. Slowly, she eased herself down onto him and the sensation of her wet silk gripping him was so intense that Shane's back teeth ached with the effort not to thrust hard and fast into her. Her face was a study in concentration, as if she, too, was finding it difficult to control her response. She caught her lower lip between her teeth and used her uninjured arm to brace herself against his chest. Late afternoon sun slanted through the skylights over the bed and picked out the blue highlights in her black hair. She'd closed her eyes and her lashes lay thick and dark against her flushed cheeks.

Shane wanted to look at her endlessly.

Then she began to move, sliding back and forth, rocking against him until he could no longer think. He moved his hands over her body, sliding them across the smoothness of her stomach and up over her breasts to trace the fragile line of her collarbones. Cupping the nape of her neck, he drew her down and slanted a deep, hard kiss across her mouth, thrusting his tongue against hers and matching the movement with his hips.

Holly groaned and angled her hips to increase the friction, the inner walls of her channel fisting hotly around him. Chase slid his hands to her bottom, cupping the perfect mounds of her cheeks as he drove himself upward. Holly used her thigh muscles to leverage herself back and forth along his cock, and her breasts teased his chest with each movement.

Reaching between their bodies, Shane found the slippery rise of her clitoris and swirled his finger over it, swallowing her soft gasps. Her movement quickened and she made an inarticulate sound of pleasure deep in her throat. Shane felt her muscles begin to contract, pulling him deeper. Her flesh clenched tightly around him, squeezing and milking him as spasms wracked her body. White-hot bolts of pure lust jack-knifed through him. He thrust deeper, intense pleasure gathering in the base of his cock and exploding outward. With a hoarse cry, he stiffened and wave after wave of release crashed over him, leaving him weak and shaking.

Slowly, he became aware that Holly lay boneless on top of him, her slender thighs still bracketing his own. She turned her face into his neck and her breath fanned his overheated skin.

"Wow," she breathed. "That was...unbelievable."

Silently, Shane agreed. Sex with Holly was off the charts. He should feel guilty about what they'd just done. She was his best friend's sister, the only daughter of a man he both esteemed and admired, *and* she outranked him. All good reasons why he should never have touched her in the first place. But he found he couldn't feel any regrets for something that he'd dreamed about doing for the past three years, since their last encounter. Even longer than that, if he was honest with himself.

He'd wanted Holly Durant since before she'd followed him into her father's wine cellar and kissed the hell out of him seven years ago. He'd been infatuated with her since the day she'd first walked into Benjamin's Drugstore as a giggling fifteen-year-old and had innocently sipped a drink while watching him work the counter.

As he'd gotten to know her better, he'd realized the sweet, southern belle image that she presented to the world was just a façade. Beneath the seemingly delicate exterior was a fiercely independent woman. Shane found the combination irresistible. She was also smart and supremely athletic. Shane had once watched her swim across the lake and back again on a dare from her brother. Nobody could tell Holly that she was incapable of doing something; she had a competitive nature and simply couldn't resist picking up the gauntlet once it had been thrown down.

Sometimes, Shane wondered if that wasn't the reason she wanted him. She liked the challenge; the thrill of the hunt. But what would she do once she finally caught him? If he gave her any indication that he felt more than just a physical attraction for her? At first she'd be thrilled, thinking she'd won. But once the novelty had worn off, he suspected that she would run as fast as possible in the opposite direction.

Sliding her to one side, he discreetly disposed of the condom and then gathered her back against him, taking care not to disturb her injured arm.

She shifted and propped her chin on her fist as she looked at him. "Hey," she said softly. "You okay?"

Afraid she would see how he felt, Shane didn't meet her eyes. Instead, he kissed her mouth and drew her back down to nestle against his chest. "Yeah. I'm perfect."

She gave a soft laugh. "Yes, you are."

Her hair tickled his jaw and he breathed in the clean scent, relishing the feel of her body pressing him into the mattress. He had a sudden moment of utter panic that this might be the only time they would have together, and he tightened his arm reflexively around her, holding her firmly against his heart.

Was this what he had felt the day of the attack, when Holly's life had been in danger? As hard as he tried, he couldn't remember anything about that day, but he suspected that what he felt now didn't come close to the sheer horror he'd experienced then. There was a part of him that couldn't even contemplate a world without Holly Durant in it.

Shane didn't know how long Holly intended to stay at the lake house, or if her parents might follow her. For all he knew, they could arrive at any time. Nor did he want to risk Holly finding out how he really felt about her. Either way, he couldn't stay. He had to leave. There was no other option. They could both be court-martialed for what they had just done. The only certainty that Shane had in his life right now was the military, and he wouldn't do anything to jeopardize that.

"Holly—"

She raised her head and laid a finger across his lips. Looking into her eyes, Shane saw that she had already anticipated his words.

"Shh," she whispered. "Don't say it. You'll ruin it."

Shane looked mutely at her. The words had to be said. Right now, she probably thought she'd won; that she'd finally caught him. But he couldn't deceive her into believing that they had any kind of a future together. They absolutely didn't.

"I know what you're going to say," she continued, "and I understand all the reasons why you think this can't work." She studied him somberly. "I won't argue with you or try to dissuade you, but I want to ask you for a favor. Will you listen?"

Shane sighed inwardly, but couldn't prevent one corner of his mouth from lifting into a reluctant smile. He didn't think there was a man alive who could say no to Holly when she had her heart set on something. So without knowing what she might ask of him, he nodded.

"I've been crazy about you for almost ten years," she finally said, as if choosing her words with careful deliberation. "You know that, right?" She gave a rueful laugh. "Forget I asked that. How could you not know?

I've thrown myself at you every chance I've had. Like now."

Shane blew out a hard breath. He *had* known Holly had a crush on him, but hearing her say she was crazy about him was like receiving a hard blow to the solar plexus, since he couldn't give her what she wanted. If she even knew what she wanted. Even if his suspicions were wrong and she really did care for him, eventually, he'd hurt her.

"You *think* you're crazy about me," he said quietly, threading his fingers through the silken strands of her hair. "But the truth is you don't even know me. You're infatuated with some romantic image that you've carried around in your head since you were a teenager, but that's not me, Holly. I'm a realist. I don't have a romantic bone in my body."

He thought she would become defensive, or act hurt. Instead, she smiled ruefully and ran the pad of her thumb over his lower lip, dragging softly at it before leaning forward to press a moist kiss on his mouth.

"Maybe you're right," she finally answered. "But that's what makes my proposition so perfect."

Shane's body tightened in wary anticipation. "Proposition?" he repeated warily. "You said you wanted to ask a favor."

She shrugged and warm color bloomed in her chest and neck. "A favor. A proposition. Call it what you want."

"I'm listening."

Holly ventured a glance at him, and Shane saw the cautious hope in her coffee-dark eyes. She chewed on her lower lip for a moment as she considered him. "Okay," she finally said, "but first you have to promise that you won't say no without at least giving this some thought. You can't deny that we have chemistry, right?"

Shane thought of what they'd just shared and gave a small huff of laughter. The periodic table didn't contain enough elements to adequately describe what happened when he and Holly came together. Pure combustion.

He rubbed a short tendril of her hair reflexively between his thumb and forefinger, admiring the texture. "I don't deny it," he replied.

"And you just said that I don't know the real you."

"Right."

"But I think I know you well enough to guess that after today, you'll insist on leaving the lake house."

Shane was silent. She did know him, it seemed.

"I don't want you to leave," Holly continued after a moment. "In fact, I'm going to propose that we both stay here and explore this…this thing between us, whatever it is."

Shane's gaze sharpened on her, certain she was joking, but her expression was somber. "Holly…"

"I won't ask you for anything you're not ready to give. I just want—I just want—" She gathered her courage. "I just want *you*. For however long you're willing to stay."

Shane studied her earnest features. "So let me make sure I understand what you're saying. You want the two of us to stay here at the lake house together, and you won't have any expectations of something permanent."

Her lips quirked into a sad sort of smile. "Right."

"And what if you want more, but I decide it's just great sex?" Shane didn't think that would ever be the case with him and Holly, but he had to ask the question.

He already knew that what he felt went beyond mere physical attraction, but he had to be certain that when the time came, she would let him go. He couldn't give her the happily ever after that she wanted, but he didn't want to hurt her.

Holly drew in a careful breath and Shane could see her struggling to find the right words. "I've thought about this more often than you could imagine. I promise that I won't ask for more than you're willing to give, and I won't make a scene if you decide you have to leave."

"Can you do that?" Shane asked quietly.

"I've been doing it for the past few years, haven't I?" She swirled a finger over the small nub of his nipple. "After my graduation party, when we spent the night together in the boathouse, I woke up and you were gone. You didn't even say goodbye."

Her tone was light, but Shane heard the soft, underlying accusation and knew he'd hurt her. But what she didn't understand was that he'd had to get out of there while he could. He'd known that if he stayed long enough for her to wake up, he'd take one look at those soulful dark eyes and he'd have been lost.

He'd have never left her if he thought there was any other way. But she'd just received her commission and her family was so damned proud of her, and she deserved more than a kid who'd opted for a GED rather than finish high school, and lived with his alcoholic father in a crappy apartment over the drugstore.

But to spend the next few weeks at the lake house with Holly, pretending they didn't have other responsibilities or demands? To spend all day, every day, in her exclusive company? To make love to her again? It was like every fantasy he'd ever had was finally coming true.

He'd be a complete idiot not to take full advantage of what she was offering. Except that in the end, he would still leave her. He hesitated.

"Your family. What if your parents come out here?"

"They won't," she assured him, sliding sensuously against him. "I told them I needed some time alone and they'll respect that." She drew one hand down the side of his body, tracing her cool fingers over the small muscles of his ribcage. When she reached his stomach and began playing with the whorl of hair beneath his navel, he couldn't prevent his body from reacting to her. "But even if they did come out here, they'd probably be thrilled to find us together. My mother always had a soft spot for you, and my dad once said he thought you had what it took to be a fine officer. He respects you."

"If anyone were to find out, they could report us. We could both be kicked out of the service for this. For myself, I could handle it, but you'd be throwing away your entire career."

Holly gave him a tolerant look. "Nobody even knows you're out here except Mitch, and I don't think he's about to call the Navy investigators and report us. Besides, we're on leave. But nobody is going to find out, Shane."

Still, he hesitated. "How long do we have?"

"Two weeks, more likely three." She paused. "I don't go before the medical board for another three weeks."

Shane grunted. "My cast comes off in three more weeks and then I return to Camp Lejeune. They'll put me on light duty for another couple of weeks but then it'll be business as usual."

For the first time since he'd enlisted, Shane found

himself less than enthusiastic about the prospect of returning to active duty. But then, he'd never had a reason to stay home. The Marines were his family and his
home, where he belonged. So why did the thought of
returning to his unit suddenly hold no appeal to him?
He wasn't sure he wanted to explore the reasons why.

In three weeks, they would both return to active duty
and any intimate relationship they had would end. Holly
was an officer and he wouldn't let her risk her career,
although a part of him suspected that after three weeks,
she'd be more than ready to say good-bye to him. It
wouldn't take her that long to realize he wasn't the man
she believed him to be.

Holly gave a soft laugh. "We're a pair, aren't we?
You with your leg and me with my arm. But I've heard
that sex releases endorphins and endorphins aid in the
healing process. So what we're doing will actually enable you to return to duty more quickly."

Shane didn't miss how she said you, not us. As in,
she had no intention of returning to active duty? He
wanted to press her further, but now wasn't the time.
He arched an eyebrow at her. "So we're doing this for
God and country, is that it?"

"Exactly." Dipping her head, Holly traced her tongue
over one flat nipple, lapping at the small bud and causing
goose bumps of sensation to chase themselves down his
spine. "Consider this your patriotic duty."

With a soft groan of surrender, Shane speared his
hands through Holly's short hair, cupping her scalp and
angling her head for a deep kiss. She gave a soft purr
of approval and slid her tongue along his, even as she
skated her hand downward, over his stomach and lower
to where he strained beneath her touch.

Before she could torment him further, Shane rolled her beneath him and raised his head just long enough to search her eyes. They were hazy with pleasure.

"Three weeks," he said, his voice rough with growing passion. "No matter what happens, this ends in three weeks. Agreed?"

"Agreed," she murmured against his mouth. "But for the next three weeks, soldier, you're all mine."

She arched her hips against him in invitation, and before his brain completely shut down, Shane silently vowed that in three weeks, he would walk away. He'd agreed to stay because he was a selfish bastard. But he'd leave because regardless of how he felt, it would be the right thing to do.

5

HOLLY WOKE UP ALONE the following morning to the sound of birdsong in the trees outside and the fragrance of freshly brewed coffee wafting up from the kitchen. She hadn't heard Shane leave and had no idea how long she'd slept. She lay in bed for several long moments and stretched luxuriously. Her body felt deliciously tender in places, and the skin around her breasts and neck was gently abraded from Shane's whiskers.

Except for when they'd gone downstairs, briefly, for something to eat, they hadn't left her bedroom. As a lover, Shane had exceeded both her memories and her expectations and Holly suspected that three weeks wouldn't be nearly enough time to get the man out of her system. Even three years wouldn't be enough. Three lifetimes, maybe.

After a hot shower, she slipped into a pair of shorts and a sleeveless top and combed her fingers through her short hair, smoothing it into place. Studying her reflection in the bathroom mirror, she thought she could detect subtle differences in her appearance. Her eyes seemed darker, filled with secret memories of their night together. Her lips were fuller, gently bruised from the force of Shane's kisses. Her skin was alabaster pale except for her cheeks, which were stained a faint pink. A tiny red mark stood out vividly at the base of her throat, just above her collarbone, where he'd sucked on her flesh. She put her fingers to it.

Shane's mark. On her skin.

She'd dreamed of possessing him for so long; of having his mouth and hands on her body, of joining herself with him. But now she knew it wasn't enough. Sex with Shane Rafferty was amazing. He drew responses from her that she hadn't known she was capable of giving, but she wanted more.

She wanted the man's heart.

A distant ringing distracted her and returning to the bedroom, she dug through her pocketbook until she found her cell phone. Seeing her parents' phone number on the display, she sighed and flipped it open.

"Hi, Mom."

Her father's deep voice filled her ear. "Are you okay?"

"Dad, I'm fine."

"But you couldn't tell us to our faces that you were going to the lake house," he said. As always, his voice was calm and controlled. His tone lacked any accusation; he was merely stating fact. Holly had never seen her dad lose his composure, not even when he'd come to see her in the hospital right after the attack. It was just one of the traits that made him a great military officer.

"I didn't think you and Mom would understand," she hedged. "I just need to be alone right now. I have some things I need to work through and Mom is always hovering. I appreciate that she just wants to help, but—"

"But she's driving you crazy. I understand."

"You do?"

"Did I ever tell you about the injury I received in Vietnam?"

Holly had heard the story, but not from her father. He never discussed that particular war and she sensed that the memories were too painful for him to even recall, never mind talk about.

"Mum told me what happened," she said quietly, "but you've never mentioned it."

"I was a young lieutenant, fresh out of officer candidate school, and we were losing young men over there faster than we could count. My father was a Marine colonel and he could have pulled some strings to keep me stateside during the war, but that's not the way the Durants operate."

Holly had heard this spiel before. The Durants never shirked their duty. They did what they needed to do, regardless of the risk or the cost.

"So you went over to Vietnam."

"That's right. I was in charge of a patrol boat that crisscrossed the Mekong Delta region. We'd been making our way upriver toward a village where Viet Cong snipers had taken out an entire company of our men just ten days earlier. We came under attack just outside of the village and we began losing men fast. I took my best sharpshooters and circled around to where we thought the snipers were hidden, and we found them." He paused. "They were just kids, Holly. Little more than babies."

"Dad…"

"I couldn't shoot, not even when one of those boys drew down on me. I couldn't do it."

Holly's chest constricted in sympathy for what her father had gone through. "So you were shot, instead."

"I was. They medivaced me back to the States and I spent eight weeks at Walter Reed hospital recovering from that injury."

Holly recalled the mass of twisted scar tissue on one side of his stomach. "But you survived."

"I did. But even after the wound healed, I wasn't fit to return to duty. Not right away."

"What did you do?"

"I went home. I thought that was where I should be, but my mother—your grandmother—almost drove me nuts. She fussed over me incessantly until finally, I had no choice but to leave."

"Where did you go?"

He chuckled. "Where else? To the lake house. Of course, in those days it wasn't much more than a two-room cottage with no electricity and no running water. But I needed to get away. I knew I wouldn't be good for much until I'd gotten my head around what had happened that day. And I couldn't return to duty until I could be certain that it would never happen again."

Holly knew he referred to his own inability to shoot the sniper. "But you did go back."

"Eventually. I couldn't let my boys down. They needed me." He was quiet for a moment. "Your troops need you, too, Holly. But not before you're ready. So you take whatever time you need. Get your head in the right place. You owe your troops that much, and you owe that to yourself."

Holly felt her throat tighten.

She wouldn't tell him about the news she had received from her doctor; that there was a good chance she'd never go back. That the military career he'd been so proud of might be over.

"Thanks, Dad."

"There's something special about the lake," he continued, his voice a little gruff with emotion. "Something peaceful and elemental. It brings out the best in people, I think."

"I love you, Dad."

"You, too. And Holly?"

"Yes?"

"It would mean a lot to me if you would come home next weekend, just for a day or so. I know your mother can be a bit much sometimes, but she has something special planned for you and I'd hate to see her disappointed."

Holly smiled. "I'll be there."

"Remember, I'm here if you need me."

Holly hung up, feeling emotionally wrung out and vulnerable after the call. She hadn't really allowed herself to think about the day of the attack. When she did, she only remembered how she'd felt about Shane when she'd thought she'd lost him. During her time at the hospital, a shrink had come to her room to evaluate her and determine if she required treatment for post traumatic stress.

Had she been afraid? Yes, she'd been terrified for Shane's safety. Did she find herself preoccupied with the events of that day? Yes, she found herself replaying those terrifying seconds when Shane had sprinted through the kill zone toward her. Did she have trouble sleeping? Yes, she had recurring nightmares that Shane hadn't survived.

In the end, they'd declared her mentally sound and

had prescribed a mild sedative for those nights when she did have trouble sleeping. But if she allowed herself to go back and recall the incident in detail, how did she really feel?

She recalled the sheer terror she'd experienced when the lead Humvees had exploded into the air, and the realization that if she and Sgt. Martinez didn't leave their truck, they might become the next target. But then her training had kicked in and she'd been so preoccupied with following protocol that there hadn't been time to feel anything. She scarcely recalled the instant when the bullet had struck her, or when the compression blast had knocked her off her feet. All she remembered was seeing Shane, bloodied and deathly still.

Shaking off the disturbing images, she picked up her camera bag and made her way down to the kitchen. Beside the coffeepot was a note, scrawled in Shane's bold handwriting.

"Down at the boathouse. Didn't want to wake you."

At least he hadn't left, she mused, pouring herself a mug of strong, black coffee and stepping outside onto the deck. The air was crisp with the scent of pine and rich, moist earth. The lake was clear and still, and she could barely hear the distant thrum of boat motors and jet-skis. The Durant family owned nearly fifty acres of land on the pristine lake, and there wasn't another cabin or house for at least a half mile in either direction, affording the family retreat complete privacy.

Holly stood at the railing and sipped her coffee, her eyes on the boathouse. What was Shane doing down there? Maybe his note had been a subtle invitation for her to join him. Maybe she would find him spread out on the small, iron bed in the guest room, waiting for her. Images of him lying back, naked and welcoming, filled her mind.

She was so caught up in her own lustful imaginings, that she didn't see the figure of a man coming around the corner of the house until he was almost directly beneath her. Startled, she sloshed hot coffee over her hand and hastily set the mug down on the railing.

"Pete?" she asked cautiously, swiping her hand across the seat of her shorts.

A stocky man stood on the lawn below the deck, with a head of thick, auburn curls and a full beard to match. He tipped his baseball cap back on his head and peered up at her.

"Holly?" His voice registered his surprise. "I didn't expect to see you out here."

She raised an eyebrow. "Who were you expecting?"

"Shane Rafferty. He called in some groceries yesterday, and I told him I'd bring them out this morning. I knocked on the front door but there was no answer. Is he here?"

"He's down in the boathouse. Sorry, I didn't hear you knock," Holly explained. "Give me a sec to put some shoes on and I'll help you bring the groceries in."

"I'd appreciate that," he said, and retreated back toward the front of the house.

Holly slid her feet into a pair of sandals and went out to the driveway where Pete's truck stood. Holly had known Pete Larson her entire life and he'd been present at more than one Durant family gathering. In fact, she was pretty sure he'd been at the lake house the night of her graduation party. He'd aged in the few years since she'd last seen him. Up close, she could see gray hair sprinkled liberally through his russet curls and laugh lines seamed his face. There were a half dozen paper sacks in the flatbed of the truck, and Pete reached in to grab one.

"Here, I'll take that," Holly offered, reaching for it.

Pete handed the bag to her, but Holly was unprepared for the weight of it, or the fact that her injured arm chose that moment to act up. She got her good arm around the top of the shopping bag, but her bad arm refused to grab it from the bottom, and the entire sack of goods slid through her grasp and split open on the driveway.

There was a moment of stunned silence as both Pete and Holly watched the juice from a broken jar of pickles seep into the ground, and cans of chili and spaghetti sauce roll in different directions. Pete reacted first, jumping forward to scoop up the escaping canned goods and redeposit them in the remaining bags. The sharp tang of pickle juice scented the air.

"That was my fault, Holly," he spluttered. "The bag was too heavy and I completely forgot about your— ah—that is—"

"It's okay, Pete," Holly assured him, absently massaging her arm. "It wasn't your fault."

"Everything okay here?"

They both turned to see Shane making his way around the corner of the house, hobbling on his cast. With one glance, he took in the broken mess on the driveway, Holly massaging her arm, and Pete's miserable expression. He smiled ruefully.

"We're quite a pair, aren't we? You should see us do the tango." His eyes slid to Holly's, and she didn't miss the quick heat that flared there, or how his gaze quickly took in every detail about her. He came forward and shook the other man's hand. "Nice to see you again, Pete. I appreciate you bringing the groceries out for me. Here, give me those two bags and come in for a cup of coffee. I'll get the rest later."

Pete looked doubtfully at Shane's leg, but at an insistent nod from Shane, handed over two bags of groceries. Shane took both bags as if they weighed nothing, and made his way carefully toward the front door.

Holly waited for Pete to grab two more bags, but when she would have taken hold of the last one, both men protested.

"Leave it, Holly," Shane commanded softly. "I'll come out and get it later."

Holly frowned. "I can handle one bag. I just wasn't ready for how heavy that other one was."

Pete gave her a friendly wink. "Never pass up an opportunity to let someone else do the work, I always say. If Shane says he'll get it, I'd let him get it."

Glancing at Shane's implacable expression, Holly blew out a hard breath of frustration. "Fine," she relented ungraciously. But as she passed Shane, she couldn't resist a softly whispered warning. "I'm the one who gives the orders around here, got it?"

But he only grinned unrepentantly and followed her and Pete into the kitchen, where he set the bags down on the counter.

"How much do I owe you?" Shane asked, pulling his wallet from his back pocket. "Did you have the spark plugs that I need in stock?"

"Sure did." Pete handed him a slip and Shane withdrew several bills and passed them to the other man.

"Here's your coffee, Pete," Holly said, setting the

coffeepot down and picking up the mug with her good hand. "You take it black, right?"

"That's right." Pete took the mug and sat down on one of the stools at the kitchen island and looked around. "I haven't been out here in a couple of years. Place still looks great."

"I haven't been here in a while, either," Holly said. She looked meaningfully at Shane. "Not since I graduated from the academy."

Pete chuckled. "That was quite a party."

"Yes, it was."

"Who'd have guessed that you'd end up in Iraq on the same base as Shane?" Pete mused, sipping his coffee. "Quite a coincidence, don't you think? And then to *both* be injured in the same battle?" He shook his shaggy head. "Unbelievable. It's almost like you were meant to be there, Holly. If you hadn't been there, Shane might not be here now."

Holly was silent, her fingers absently rubbing the edge of the counter. She didn't dare look at Shane. If she hadn't been there, Shane never would have been injured. He'd only abandoned his turret gun because he'd thought she was in danger.

Oblivious to the sudden tension in the room, Pete blundered on. "I hear the town of Chatham is planning a parade in your honor."

She raised shocked eyes to his. "*What?* No, that can't be right. Why would they do that? I didn't even do anything!"

"You saved this man's life, didn't you? As far as the town is concerned, you're a local hero."

Holly's head was spinning. This had to be a mistake. Anyone who knew the facts could see that she wasn't a hero. Just the opposite, in fact. She'd almost gotten Shane killed!

"When is the parade scheduled?" asked Shane mildly.

Holly looked at him, but if he was upset about the news, nothing showed on his face.

"Hell, from what I hear, it's more than just a parade; it's a whole day of festivities," Pete continued enthusiastically. "The parade just kicks the whole thing off, next Saturday."

"Wait. Next Saturday? As in a week from tomorrow? That can't be right. My parents would have told me. Someone would have told me. There's no way they would try to keep this a secret and then spring it on me at the last minute." She turned anguished eyes to Shane. "Would they?"

"Well, I don't know," Shane drawled. "Maybe they thought you'd split town if you found out. Maybe they thought you'd take off and go hide out at the lake house."

Holly groaned. "My dad called this morning and asked if I'd consider coming home for the weekend. He said that Mom had something special planned."

Pete chuckled. "I guess the hell she does. There's going to be a barbeque on the town common, and they've organized all kinds of activities including a bake sale, a pie-eating contest, a dunk tank, and that's just what I can remember from the fliers. There'll be a barn dance that night with live music, and more food." Pete chuckled. "I wouldn't be surprised if they turn it into an annual event...*Holly Durant Day*. Has a nice ring to it, don't you think?"

"No," Holly grumbled.

"I think it has an excellent ring to it," Shane protested. "And I personally think you deserve the recognition."

Holly stared at him. A muscle worked in his lean jaw, but there was no denying the sincerity in his voice.

"You do?" she asked.

"Holly, you were shot and nearly blown to bits trying to save me. What you did was incredibly brave." He was staring hard at her now, twin patches of color riding high on his lean cheeks. "When I think what could have happened—"

The expression in his hazel eyes mesmerized Holly. She could hardly breathe. He was looking at her as if she were the most precious thing in the world.

"But I'm here," she said softly. "And so are you."

"And that's my cue to leave," declared Pete, looking embarrassed. He took a hefty swig of his coffee and rose to his feet. "Good seeing you kids. I'll just leave that bag of groceries on the front steps, but don't forget about it. Feel better. I'll see you at the parade."

Holly barely noticed him leave. "We haven't talked about it," she said to Shane. "The attack, I mean."

Shane had been unpacking the grocery bags and now his fist tightened around a hapless bunch of asparagus. Moving around the counter, Holly covered his hand with her own.

"I know you blame yourself for what happened that day, but don't. None of it was your fault."

Dropping the vegetables, Shane turned to her and Holly saw the stark vulnerability and frustration in his eyes. "But that's just it. I don't *remember* that day. I can't recall a single goddamned detail of what happened." He gave a bitter laugh. "I can't tell you why I left my gun or why I thought I needed to save you—if that's even what I was doing." He ran a shaking hand over his face. "But Jesus, at night…"

Holly laid a hand on his chest, feeling the heavy thump of his heart beneath her palm. She didn't need to ask what kept him up at night; if his nightmares were anything like the ones she'd been having, it was a wonder he could even close his eyes.

He turned abruptly away and began shoving items into the refrigerator. Holly watched him for a moment.

"The tango, huh?" she finally asked. Anything to get his mind off his own tormented thoughts.

"What?" He glanced at her over his shoulder, his expression confused.

"You said to Pete that he should see us do the tango." She waggled her eyebrows at him. "Is that what they're calling it these days?"

He closed the fridge door and turned back to her, bracing his hands on the counter. He didn't return her smile. "How bad is the arm?" he finally asked. "And I want the truth."

For a moment, Holly felt off-balance. She couldn't find the words to answer him. Didn't want to answer him. Didn't want to admit to herself that her injury limited what she could do.

She shrugged and strove for a casual tone. "It's not that bad. I mean, it's only been a month, so I shouldn't expect a full recovery so soon. I have a follow-up appointment in a couple of weeks. Maybe the doctors will have better news then."

"Let me take a look." His voice was low and brooked no argument, and before she realized what she was doing, Holly extended her injured arm toward him. He took it in both of his hands and very carefully turned it toward the light.

Holly looked away. The scars were angry red and there was still some residual swelling where the bullet had ripped through her flesh. Because of the location of the break, the doctors hadn't been able to put a cast on her arm. Instead, they'd pieced her bone back together with a metal plate and a series of screws, which would remain permanently in her arm. There was no question the area was ugly to look at, and Holly wished she had the courage to pull her arm free from Shane's grasp.

"Another inch higher and your shoulder socket would have been destroyed," Shane murmured, stroking his fingers lightly over the damaged area. "Does it hurt?"

She shrugged. "A little."

"Liar."

Holly raised her eyes to his and saw humor and compassion and something else lingering in their moss green depths. Her heart began to drum faster in her chest.

"What do you mean?"

"You massage your arm whenever you think nobody is watching, and last night you made little moaning sounds in your sleep." He continued to rub the area with his thumb, as if he could work the pain out.

"I do? I did?"

"Mmm-hmm." He turned her arm, examining it from different angles. "Do you remember getting hit?"

The way he was stroking her skin and talking to her in that low, sexy voice, it was a wonder Holly could remember her own name. She shook her head. "Not really. I remember feeling a hard slap against my arm, and then a second later the explosion knocked me off my feet. You have a strange expression on your face right now. What's wrong?"

Shane lowered her arm and swiped a hand across his eyes. "I don't know. It's probably nothing. I just wish I could remember. I don't recall being shot. I have no memory of the explosion or of you dragging me to safety, or being airlifted out of there." He pinched the bridge of his nose. "It's like someone took a giant eraser and just wiped the slate clean for that day. But there's something there, I can feel it. Something important about that day, if I could just freaking *remember*."

Reaching out, Holly laid a hand on his arm. "You will. Eventually. This is just your body's way of dealing with the trauma, but eventually I'm sure you'll recall what happened that day."

"The worst part is knowing that I'm responsible for what happened to you." His voice was low and Holly could hear the self-loathing in his tone. "I deserve to remember what happened, if only to replay it again and again in my head."

Holly stared at him in disbelief. "Why? As a form of punishment?" She gave a bitter laugh. "Trust me, it's not all it's cracked up to be. I relive that day enough for the both of us. I wouldn't wish that kind of self-flagellation on anyone."

"Tell me what happened. Tell me everything that you remember about it."

Holly shuddered. "I'd rather not."

To her surprise, Shane gathered her close, his hands stroking over her back. "I'm sorry. I'm a bastard to even suggest it, but I thought if I could hear it in your words, that maybe it would trigger something. Maybe I would finally *remember*."

Holly nuzzled into his strength and warmth, relishing this new closeness to him. She didn't want to ruin it by dredging up the events of that horrible day. "Maybe later," she hedged. "But not right now."

He made a sound that could have been either frustration or capitulation. "You're right. This isn't the time or place."

"What were you doing in the boathouse, before Pete showed up?"

"I thought if I could get the boat running, I'd take you out on the lake, but I think the spark plugs need replacing. I asked Pete to bring some out with him." He fished through the nearest grocery bag and pulled out a small packet, holding it triumphantly. "Give me a couple of minutes, and I'll have the motor purring like a kitten."

Holly brightened at the prospect of spending the day with Shane on the lake. Her parents kept an older boat that Mitch and Shane had often used when they were younger. The motor was temperamental, but Shane had always managed to keep it running.

"Sounds wonderful. I'll pack us a lunch."

Shane took the new spark plugs and left, while Holly pulled out the makings for sandwiches. She looked up, surprised, when Shane reappeared a few moments later.

"That was fast," she began, but broke off when she saw Shane's face. "What's wrong?"

He wore an expression of deep concern, and Holly saw that he still carried the spark plugs in one hand. "I know this is a stupid question, but were you down in the boathouse by any chance?"

"Me?" Holly asked in surprise. "No, why?"

In fact, the last time she'd been inside the boathouse had been at her college graduation party, when she'd followed Shane to bed. Unless he was there, Holly had no reason to enter the little building.

Shane scrubbed a hand across his head. "Jesus."

Holly frowned and set down the utensil she'd been holding. "What is it? Is something wrong?"

"Yeah. I was messing around with the boat motor yesterday, trying to get it running. I realized it needed new spark plugs, so I put the cover back on and I haven't looked at it again until just now."

"So?"

"So if I hadn't opened the engine compartment to replace the plugs…if I'd just inserted the key and tried to start the boat…"

He looked a little sick and Holly came quickly around the side of the counter. "What? What would have happened?"

"Someone tampered with the engine, Holly. I swear I left everything exactly the way it should be, but when I opened the engine compartment just now… Someone had disconnected the fuel line and put it up on the engine block. Then the electric coil was disconnected from the distributor, and was lying up against the block."

Holly shook her head helplessly, but something tight and fearful fisted in her stomach. "I'm sorry, I don't follow. What does that mean?"

"If I **had tried** to start the engine, electricity would arc right **to the block and** cross over the gas line, causing an **explosion that** would probably destroy the boat, level the **boathouse,** and seriously hurt or kill whoever was in there."

Holly stared at him, unable to process the words.

"What are you saying? That someone tried to kill you?"

Shane gripped Holly's good arm. "Do you know anyone who might have done this? *Think,* Holly."

Holly shook her head. "I don't know. I can't think of anyone. It's been so long since I've been out here... there's a family farther down the lake who had a bunch of young boys. They'd be teenagers now. Maybe one of them did it as a prank."

Shane released her and turned away to rake a hand over his hair. He looked a little wild-eyed and every muscle in his body was tightly coiled. "If this was a prank, it was in pretty poor taste. Someone could have been killed."

"You didn't notice anything unusual about the engine when you were down there this morning, before Pete showed up?"

Shane shook his head. "I didn't even look at the engine. I was just washing the boat out so that we could use it later."

"So this happened sometime during the last twenty-four hours?"

"Yes. I didn't even think to lock the boathouse overnight. This property isn't easy to access, so someone would have to deliberately go out of their way to get to the boat." His voice was grim. "My guess is that whoever did this came in by water; I checked the entire area around the boathouse and found no trace of footprints. How many people do you know who might come to visit the lake house on their boat?"

"Shane, my parents know every family on this side of the lake and they all have boats. Any one of them has pulled up at the dock one time or another, but I can't think of a single person who might have been capable of tampering with the engine."

Shane blew out a hard breath. "Okay. A stranger, then. Or someone with an ax to grind. Is your dad at odds with anyone right now?"

Holly shook her head, bewildered. "No. I mean, I don't think so. You know my dad. Everyone loves him. He has no enemies."

Shane glanced out toward the lake, his expression troubled. "I don't like how this feels. Until we find out who did this, I don't want you going out alone, got it?"

"I'll call the police and report it," Holly said. "Maybe there've been other incidents around the lake, although my gut feeling is that this was just a malicious prank. I wonder if whoever did this even knew what would happen if someone did try to start the engine."

"They knew," Shane said darkly, his hand fisting compulsively around the packet of spark plugs. "From now on, you keep the doors locked at all times and turn on the security system, even during the day. I don't like the thought of some punk lurking around the property. If someone could do this, who knows what else they're capable of doing."

"We've had break-ins at the boathouse before. Once, they stole all our boating equipment and stripped the boat of its electronics. But it's been a long time since we've had any problems with vandalism." She indicated the spark plugs in his hand. "Do you still want to take the boat out?"

Shane snorted and tossed the package onto the counter. "Without being certain that the vandals didn't tamper with anything else on board, that's not a chance I'm willing to take."

"What about the row boat? I'm guessing they didn't tamper with that?"

Shane arched one dark eyebrow. "I'm guessing you're not volunteering to do the rowing."

Holly laughed and encircled one of his biceps with her hands. "There's absolutely nothing wrong with your arms."

That was the truth; he looked as if he hefted tanks for a living, and even after four weeks of recovery and recuperation, his skin was warm and golden, as if he had been steeped in the desert sun.

"Okay," he relented. "I'll row, but you're packing us a *really* good lunch."

"Deal." She slanted him a wicked grin. "I'll put a call into the police right now, and then pack a cooler. If there's one thing the military has taught me, it's never to let a soldier go hungry. Trust me. I'll satisfy your appetite."

6

IT WAS JUST BEFORE noon as Shane watched Holly walk out onto the dock where he had the rowboat waiting. He couldn't get his mind off the fact that someone had dared to break into the boathouse and tamper with the boat's motor. Just thinking about what could have happened made him go cold inside. What if Holly had been on board? As it was, he wouldn't let her inside the boathouse, and had tied the dingy alongside the dock. She'd called the local police and they'd asked her and Shane to come down to the station later that day to file a report. They had seemed to agree with Holly's assertion that the incident was most likely a malicious prank.

Shane had his doubts.

He'd spent the better part of the morning trying to consider all the possibilities, including terrorism. What if someone knew Holly was at the lake house? What if they wanted to eliminate her and send a message to other American service men and women? Just the thought sent chills through him. In the next instant, he silently berated himself for being overly dramatic. Looking at the lake's surrounding woodlands, he had a tough time imagining that anything bad could happen in such an idyllic place. But he'd keep his guard up, just the same.

He'd carried down a small cooler and a tote bag for her earlier, and stowed them in the front of the little craft, but Holly had claimed she'd forgotten something and had run back up to the house. Now he saw her camera bag in one hand and had to suppress a groan. His earliest memories of Holly had been of her following him around with a camera, snapping pictures whenever she thought he wasn't looking.

She wore a short, bright yellow sundress that contrasted warmly with her pale skin, and a wide-brimmed straw hat that cast sun-dappled shadows over her face. Her long, slim legs were bare and as he helped her down into the boat, he caught a glimpse of pink panties. He'd been preoccupied with thoughts of the vandalism, but now he groaned inwardly, knowing that brief flash of fabric would haunt him all morning.

He waited until she'd settled herself onto the seat facing him, before untying the line and pushing them away from the dock. He had to extend his injured leg so that it rested beneath Holly's seat, and they were so close their knees almost bumped. When he leaned forward to grasp the oars, he became distracted by the way her short skirt draped over her bare legs.

"Why did you have to wear a dress?" he grumbled, pulling smoothly on the oars and drawing them out onto the stillness of the lake.

"Why not?" She smiled serenely. "After months of wearing camouflage and combat boots, it feels wonderful to wear something feminine. Do you have a problem with my wearing a dress?"

He eyed her bare knees. "It just seems impractical, that's all."

"Mmm. Maybe to you, but to me it seems perfect." She leaned forward and kissed him, letting her lips linger against his in a way that made him go hard beneath his shorts. Too soon, she pulled away and rearranged her skirt over her thighs. "So where are we going?"

Shane was glad he wore a pair of dark sunglasses, as he couldn't prevent his gaze from drifting to the shadowed vee between her legs, where her dress fell away and he imagined he could see a bit of pink fabric. "There's a little island not far from here, where Mitch and I used to go to get away."

"Ah. As in…away from me?"

Most definitely away from Holly. Going to the island had always been Shane's idea, since it was the one place he could be guaranteed not to run into Holly. Even at sixteen, she'd been a temptation that he'd found difficult to resist. The only way he'd succeeded was to put as much distance as possible between them.

"Not just you," he fibbed. "Away from your parents, away from my dad…just away."

"What did you do once you got away?" She tipped her head and considered him. "If it were anyone but you and Mitch, I'd say you went out there to smoke dope. Or drink."

Shane laughed. "Yeah, well, we definitely did some drinking out there, and some smoking, too. But just cigarettes, not dope. Mostly, we just hung out. We brought our fishing poles and used those as an excuse to basically do nothing."

Holly looked disappointed. "Sounds boring. At least

tell me that you had some girly magazines or something."

There *had* been some magazines, as Shane recalled. Some shockingly graphic magazines that had made his young body go tight with lust, and guaranteed he would have erotic dreams later that night in the boathouse. Those dreams nearly all involved Holly, and he would wake up spent and wet and aching for her.

He gave her a benign smile in answer, and continued rowing. He set a leisurely pace, not overexerting himself but ensuring they'd reach the island before Holly had a chance to become bored. He watched as she draped a hand over the edge of the boat and trailed her fingers through the water, and then drizzled the moisture down her neck. For the first time, Shane noticed the small mark at the base of her neck. He remembered drawing the tender flesh into his mouth and sucking on it. Seeing the evidence of their night together gave him a fierce sense of possessiveness.

"Oh, that feels good," she sighed, stroking her damp fingers across her skin. "I should have worn a bathing suit."

"Didn't you bring one with you?"

"Nope." She gave him a secretive smile. "I guess I'll have to skinny-dip if I want to swim. But you'll only be able to watch, since you can't get your cast wet."

"Jesus." Shane swallowed hard at the image of Holly, naked and dripping with water. He pulled harder on the oars. He could see the island in the distance and if he put his back into it, they could be there in under ten minutes.

Holly took one look at his expression and laughed, but Shane thought she seemed just as eager as he did to reach their destination. Soon, he beached the small craft on the shore of the small island and stepped out onto the sand.

She looked doubtfully at his toes where they protruded from the cast. "Maybe you should cover that with something," she suggested. "If sand gets in there, you're going to be very uncomfortable."

He was going to be uncomfortable, regardless, but the idea of wearing a sock or a plastic sleeve over the cast was even more repugnant.

"I'll be fine," he assured her. "It's a swim cast, so contrary to what you said about my not being able to follow you into the water, I actually can. So if sand gets in there, I'll just rinse it out." He grabbed the tote bag and the cooler, and opted to leave his cane in the boat. Ignoring Holly's protests, he extended his free hand to her. "Here, give me your hand. The ground is a little uneven."

Holly frowned and looked to where his cane lay on the bottom of the boat. "Shane, I'm not going to be responsible for you losing your balance and ending up with a cast on your other leg. Take your cane. I can manage on my own."

He gave her a look and extended his hand again. He didn't miss how she rolled her eyes, but she obediently slid her hand into his as he led her away from the water and deeper into the dense growth of the small island.

"Where are we going?"

"To the other side of the island," he replied, "but it's not very far. We could have rowed around to the other side, but this is actually quicker."

Even as he spoke, the trees cleared and they found themselves approaching a deep cove. The lake lapped gently at a small, sandy shore with outcroppings of rock. The tiny inlet was secluded and quiet, and sunlight dappled the water and turned the surface into a million glittering diamonds.

"Oh, how pretty!" Holly exclaimed. "How come I never knew about this place growing up?"

Even as she spoke, she began rummaging through her bag. Pulling her camera out, she sat down in the sand and cradled it in her lap as she twisted one lens off and carefully replaced it with another. Shane watched her, noting how she did most of the work with her good hand, and used her injured arm to balance rather than maneuver the camera. When she attempted to pick the heavy telephoto lens up using her left hand, he could see she had trouble getting a good grip on it. He carefully looked away, pretending not to notice her difficulty.

Holly's injury was worse than she'd let on. Shane had seen enough combat related wounds to know she'd suffered nerve damage. He set the cooler and bag down on the sand, forcing himself to behave naturally. But he didn't trust his own expression, so he stood with his back to her and pretended to look out over the cove. He sensed when she came up beside him, holding the camera in her good hand.

"This is beautiful, Shane." Raising the camera, she fumbled for a second until she got a good grip, and then swiftly snapped several frames of the cove. "The water is so clear that you can see the pebbles on the lake bottom. I can see why you and Mitch used to come out here. Does anyone else ever use the island?"

"Not that I'm aware."

"Did you ever bring girls out here?"

Shane looked at her, surprised. "Me? No. I think

Mitch might have brought a date out here on one or two occasions, but you'll have to ask him about that. I never brought anyone."

He'd wanted too, though. He'd imagined bringing Holly out here on more than one occasion, but he'd have never actually done it. He didn't have the courage. At least, not back then.

"I'm glad I'm your first," she said. Then, as if sensing his discomfort, she quickly changed the subject. "Here, I brought an old quilt that we can spread out on the sand."

Replacing the camera, she pulled a folded blanket out of the tote bag, but made no protest when Shane took it from her and shook it out on the ground. He watched as she kicked off her sandals and lowered herself onto the blanket, tucking her bare legs beneath her. After a moment, Shane dropped down beside her.

"So what did you and my brother talk about when you came out here?" she asked.

He shrugged. "I really don't remember."

She rested her chin on her shoulder and considered him for a moment. "I'll never forget the first time I saw you at the drugstore. The girls at Chatham Hall were already talking about the mysterious new guy in town, so I had to see for myself. I thought you were the most beautiful boy I had ever seen."

Shane gave a bark of surprised laughter. "Me? I don't think anyone has ever described me as beautiful. As I recall, I was an angry kid with a bad attitude."

"That just added to your mystique." She removed her hat and placed it on the blanket beside her. "Why were you angry?"

Shane didn't want to talk about his adolescence. For

the first time that he could recall, he felt…at peace. Talking about those years would only dredge up feelings better left undisturbed. He didn't expect Holly would understand what he'd been through or how it had colored everything he did.

"Trust me, there's no mystique where I'm concerned," he said wryly. "Everything about me is right there on the surface."

"Okay," Holly said softly. "I understand if you don't want to talk about it."

"There's nothing to talk about," he insisted, but he could see she didn't believe him.

He watched warily as she rose to her knees and walked on them across the blanket toward him. He had a brief glimpse of her pink panties when she hiked up her skirt to straddle him, and his breath left his lungs in a whoosh as her warm thighs bracketed his own. She looped her arms lightly around his neck and leaned back a bit to look at him.

"You don't always have to be so strong, you know," she finally said.

"Is that an order?" he asked, in an attempt to inject some humor into a conversation that was becoming increasingly uncomfortable.

Holly smiled. "Soldier, when I give you an order, you'll know it. Now kiss me."

"Ah," he replied, feeling his mouth curve upward. "That sounded suspiciously like an order."

"Smart *and* gorgeous," she teased, and then she kissed him.

Her lips were incredibly soft and she tasted sweet, as if she'd recently sucked on a piece of hard candy. Shane couldn't believe how much he'd missed the feel of her mouth against his, even after a few short hours. She made a purring sound of approval and hitched herself higher on his lap, tunneling her fingers through his hair as she licked and sucked at his mouth. Angling her head, she deepened the kiss, even as her soft breasts pressed against his chest and she rocked softly against his groin.

Shane heard himself moan and reaching behind her, he cupped her luscious rear in his hands, feeling the heat of her body through the thin fabric of her sundress. He helped her move against him, but it wasn't enough. He wanted to reach beneath her skirts and drag the pink panties from her body, and then lower her onto his aching shaft.

"See what I mean about wearing a dress?" she asked on a soft gasp, hitching herself higher on his lap, until she was pressed fully against his aching erection. "Very practical."

She pressed moist kisses along his jaw as her fingers fisted in his T-shirt. "Take this off. I need to see you."

Reaching over his head, Shane grabbed a fistful of shirt and dragged it upward, pulling it over his head and tossing it onto the blanket. Her hands were everywhere, stroking across his chest and shoulders and then over his back, while she murmured soft words of delight. Her hands returned to skim over his stomach to the fastening of his shorts.

"You didn't happen to bring any of those condoms with you, did you?" she asked breathlessly.

He shoved a hand into his front pocket and withdrew several foil packets. He shrugged when he saw the amused look she gave him. "Hey, I was hopeful."

"I want you naked," she breathed. "Fast."

Her hands fumbled with the snap of his jeans and Shane realized they were trembling. Flicking the snap open, he turned with Holly in his arms until she lay beneath him on the blanket. She gazed up at him, her irises so dark that he had trouble distinguishing her pupils. Her pink lips were parted and her breath came in soft pants.

"You are so damned pretty," he rasped and lowered his head to her mouth, pressing past her lips until their teeth scraped together. She made a soft sound of pleasure and arched against him, one hand at the nape of his neck to hold him in place.

Dragging her skirt upward, Shane's fingers encountered the slippery silk of her panties and he smoothed his hand over the fabric, feeling the heat that she radiated. She wriggled beneath him and opened her thighs in silent encouragement, and Shane slipped his fingers beneath the fragile barrier until he held her in his hand.

"Yes," she breathed into his mouth. "Touch me."

With a smothered groan, Shane delved gently through her soft folds, her slick heat sparking something raw and primitive inside him. Swiftly he pushed her dress up until her midriff and hips were exposed. He kissed his way across the framework of her ribs to the softness of her abdomen, lingering over the delicate whorl of her navel. She shifted restlessly beneath him, spearing her fingers through his hair as he dipped his head lower and breathed in her feminine scent.

Hooking his thumbs into the waistband of the pink panties, he dragged them down her legs. Holly helped him by kicking them free of her body until finally, nothing lay between them.

Shane let himself admire her for a brief instant before

he pressed a kiss against her mons, just beneath the small triangle of dark curls. Her breathing quickened and her fingers rubbed against his scalp. Sliding his hands beneath her bottom, Shane lifted her and licked boldly along her cleft. She gave a strangled cry of pleasure and gripped his head, and Shane took her fully in his mouth. He lapped her essence, relishing the taste of her, before spearing his tongue inside her, using it to torment both of them. She writhed against his face and when he glanced up, he could see her body was bowed with tension, her eyes closed and her face taut. The sight of her wracked beneath his mouth was incredibly erotic.

He softened his tongue, flattening it as he massaged her clit, providing just enough pressure to make her moan but not enough to give her the release she craved. At the same time, he eased a finger into her clenching tightness and then followed it with a second finger, thrusting gently as he teased her with his tongue.

He knew she was on the brink of coming. Her legs stiffened and her muscles clenched, and she made a low noise of pleasure-pain deep in her throat. Shane flicked her clit hard with his tongue and she fractured, her mouth opening on a keening cry as deep shudders washed over her.

He didn't give her time to recover. Pushing his shorts free, he quickly covered himself with a condom before he rolled Holly onto her stomach on the blanket. She turned her face to the side, gasping softly. Shane ran his hand along the elegant length of her back, admiring the supple muscles along her spine. Grasping her hips, he raised them slightly and she accommodated him by bending her knees and arching toward him. Shane positioned himself at her opening and slowly fed his length into her, inch by exquisite inch, gritting his teeth as her flesh gripped him tightly.

When he was fully buried in her heat, he came over her, bracing his weight on one arm as he thrust into her. He pressed kisses wherever he could, along her shoulders and her spine, against the nape of her neck and her throat. He swirled his tongue along the curve of her ear and whispered to her how good she felt. Using his thighs to spread her wider, he reached around to her front and dipped his fingers to the spot where they were joined.

"I want you to come again," he growled.

"I can't," she protested weakly.

"You can." He scraped his teeth across her nape, felt her shiver. "You will."

He swirled his finger over her clitoris as he thrust deeply inside her welcoming flesh.

"You are so fucking gorgeous down there," he whispered, biting gently on the lobe of her ear. "I loved eating you, loved watching you come in my mouth."

Her breathing quickened and a gush of moisture flowed over his cock and hand. She rotated her hips against him. "Oh, yeah," he said, his voice husky with passion. "You're so wet. Can you feel me inside you?" He withdrew almost completely and then sank strongly back into her. She gave a soft moan and beneath his fingers, Shane felt the small nub of her clitoris swell and grow hard. "That's it," he purred, increasing the rhythm of his fingers as he stroked her with his cock. "Oh, man, you are so tight. I'm not sure I can last."

He pumped harder, faster. Holly pushed back against him as he tormented her with his fingers, and her breathing hitched.

"Oh my God," she panted in desperation, "I'm going to…"

"I'm right here," he rasped, and when he felt her inner muscles clamp ruthlessly around his flesh, felt her body spasm and shudder with release, the force of his climax caused his back to arch and wrenched a hoarse cry from deep within him.

Holly collapsed against the quilt, her shoulders heaving. Shane knelt there for a moment, dragging air into his lungs as he struggled to regain his equilibrium. After a moment he rose and made his way to the edge of the water where he quickly cleaned himself off and discreetly disposed of the condom. As he turned, he saw Holly watching him through slumberous eyes. She had pulled the skirt of her dress back down so that her luscious rear was covered, but knowing that she was bare and likely still quivering beneath the thin material gave Shane a deep sense of satisfaction.

Dragging his shorts back on, he opened the small cooler they had brought with them and withdrew a bottle of cold water. As he eased himself down onto the blanket beside her, he twisted the cap off and handed the bottle to her, watching as she took several gulps.

"Mmm, I was thirsty," she murmured and tried to hand the water back to Shane, but he shook his head and dropped a kiss against her shoulder.

Then he lay back, bent his arms beneath his head, and closed his eyes. He sensed rather than heard Holly shift, and then felt the warm length of her body as she lay beside him and rested her head on his shoulder. He cracked one eyelid open and looked down at her. Her short hair was tousled and her face was still flushed. She smiled at him in contentment and Shane felt something in his chest tighten.

"No one's ever done that before," she murmured.

"Done what?" He didn't want to know. Didn't want to think of her with anyone else, doing the things she had done with him.

"Talked to me like that during…" She broke off with an embarrassed laugh.

Turning on his side, Shane propped his head on his hand and considered her. "But you liked it." He couldn't keep the male satisfaction out of his voice. He dropped his voice to a seductive whisper. "And every word was true. You tasted delicious."

He watched as a flush of color seeped into her cheeks and she rolled against him to hide her face against his side. "I don't know how you can be like that," she whispered.

"Like what?"

"So…uninhibited."

He gave a rueful laugh and smoothed a lock of dark hair back from her ear. "Trust me, with you it's easy."

Raising her face, she gave him a slightly reproachful look. "Why did you leave without saying good-bye?"

Shane didn't pretend to misunderstand her. He knew she referred to the night of her graduation party, when they'd made love in the boathouse. He sighed. "You wouldn't understand."

"Try me."

Shane scrubbed a hand over his face. "That night was a mistake, Holly. I left because I didn't want you getting the wrong idea."

Holly frowned. "About what?"

"Look, I knew you had feelings for me. I took

advantage of you that night and it was wrong. Part of the reason I didn't stay was due to my own guilt, and part of it was because I didn't want to give you any false hope. I thought if I left, then you'd realize our being together was a mistake, too, and move on with your life."

"Oh."

"And the other part..." He hesitated. "The other part was because I didn't *want* to say good-bye to you. I wanted to stay with you."

"Oh." He watched as she digested this bit of information. "So what you're really saying is that after all this time, nothing has really changed."

Now it was Shane's turn to look puzzled. "What do you mean?"

"In three weeks, you're going to leave again, and we'll be right back where we started."

7

HOLLY WATCHED SHANE'S face carefully as she said the words, but to her immense disappointment, he didn't disagree with her. If he felt any regret about the inevitable end of their affair, nothing showed on his face. With a sigh of regret, Holly stared up through the leafy branches at the sky. The frustrating part was knowing that Shane wanted her. She knew he cared about her. No man could touch a woman the way he'd touched her unless he had feelings for her.

Rolling her head on the quilt, she looked over at him. "Do you remember the first time we met?"

A smile touched Shane's mouth. "Yeah. I was working the counter at Benjamin's and you came in with your ridiculous friends."

Holly gasped in mock outrage. "Ridiculous? We weren't ridiculous."

"You absolutely were. Do you think I didn't know why you came into the drugstore every afternoon? You all stood at the counter and stared at me with those simpering smiles, and every time I turned away you'd *laugh*."

"We thought you were gorgeous, but you were so bad-tempered and you glowered at us whenever we tried to say anything to you."

"Like I said—ridiculous."

"So what did you think of me?" she asked softly.

His gaze slid to hers in warning. "Holly…"

"Tell me." She rolled toward him and threw one leg over his strong thighs and an arm across his bare chest, pinning him to the quilt. "I won't let you up until you do."

To her surprise, he captured her leg and drew it up higher, and then slid his hand along her thigh until he encountered the bare skin of her hip.

"In that case," he muttered, turning his face toward her.

He was going to kiss her, but Holly knew that if he did, there would be no more conversation. She pressed her fingers over his mouth to stop him.

"Tell me," she insisted softly.

Shane released her leg, blowing out a hard breath. "Fine. I thought you were the prettiest girl I had ever seen."

"You did?"

"Mmm-hmm. Your hair was so long and sleek, and it shimmered whenever you shook it. Which was all the time."

Holly laughed. "I was very vain about my hair in those days."

"Why did you cut it off?"

She made a face. "Long hair isn't practical in the military. I like it short."

"I do, too."

"So you thought I was pretty," she continued. "What else?"

He laughed in bemusement. "I don't know. I was a kid. I met Mitch when he came to work at the drugstore and the first time he invited me back to your house and I realized you were his sister, I almost walked out and never came back."

"Really?" This was getting good. "Why?"

Shane sat up, disentangling himself from her limbs. "Okay, you know what? This is a stupid conversation. You *know* why. Because even back then, I wanted you and it didn't help that you pretty much threw yourself at me every chance you got. I was trying to do the right thing, but you made it very difficult."

"I threw myself at you *once*," Holly said indignantly. "On Christmas Eve. Never before that. And you still rejected me."

"It took every bit of strength I had to push you away," he muttered darkly. "You have no idea how close you came to being violated in your father's wine cellar that night."

Holly tipped her head, wondering at his choice of words. She didn't recall feeling violated at all. Aroused and frustrated, but not violated. "What do you think of me now?"

Shane slanted her a sardonic look. "I think I just demonstrated how I feel about you."

Holly took a hasty swallow of water to hide her disappointment. What they'd just shared had been amazing, it had only been physical. But what had she expected? A declaration of love? He'd made it clear that he believed any relationship between them couldn't work, but what she wanted to know was *why*.

"You said earlier that you were an angry kid," she finally said. "Was it because of what happened with your parents?"

He looked surprised. "Mitch told you?"

Holly snorted. "Mitch never told me anything. I was the annoying little sister, remember? He was extremely loyal to you. Whatever secrets you two shared, he'll never tell anyone."

"So what do you know about my parents?"

She'd heard rumors, of course, but as much as she'd pressed Mitch to tell her details about where Shane had come from and what his family was like, he'd tersely told her that she'd have to ask Shane. Which, of course, she'd never dared to do. Until now.

"When we were in school," she began carefully, "there were rumors that your mom ran off with another man and your father turned to the bottle. Is that true?"

Shane scooped up a handful of sand and let it trickle through his fingers. "I wish it were as simple as that." He was quiet for several long seconds, as if debating how much to share. "My father came from nothing, but he knew thoroughbreds. He grew up working at a racetrack in Kentucky, walking and exercising the horses. Eventually, he got into training and was invited to work at one of the best stables in Lexington."

"I knew he was a horse trainer," Holly admitted. "I don't know a lot about thoroughbred racing, but I've heard that good trainers often go on to open their own stables."

Shane gave a bitter laugh. "My dad could have done that. By the time he was in his early twenties he'd already made a name for himself in the racing world. But there was a reason why he wanted to stay at this particular stable. He was in love with the owner's daughter."

Holly looked sharply at him, but Shane's gaze was focused inward. "What happened?"

"Like I said, he knew thoroughbreds and he knew how to make them respond to his touch. My mother was young, barely out of high school and although her parents appreciated my father's skill with their horses, they disapproved of him as a suitable husband for their daughter. So she and my dad ran away together."

"Your mother was the owner's daughter?"

"Yes." Shane blew out a hard breath. "They were young and stupid. They had no money and nowhere to go." He snorted. "They thought they could live on love until I came along, and then things really got tough."

"What about your grandparents? Your mother's parents? They had money. Couldn't they help?"

"They offered, but at a price. My mother was welcome to return home, but only if she came without me or my father. So she stayed with my dad, and they struggled. My mother's family made sure that my father wouldn't find work at any stable or racetrack in Kentucky. So they came to Virginia and he found a job, but the money wasn't enough to give my mother the things she craved." He angled his head and looked at Holly. "She loved my father and me, but she resented the sacrifices she had to make."

Holly laid a hand on his arm. "She *left* you?"

"In a manner of speaking. By the time I was a teenager, she and my father argued constantly, usually about money. She used to threaten to leave him and go back to Kentucky. He worked three jobs to try and give her the lifestyle she was accustomed to, including a membership to the local country club and a fast car, but it wasn't enough. He was never around and she spent too much time alone." He plucked at a loose thread on the quilt. "I was fourteen when she came home late one night from the club. She'd had too much to drink. I've never seen my father so angry, mostly because she'd driven herself home. They argued, and before he could stop her, she took off again in the car. About a half mile from the house, she hit a tree and died instantly."

Holly was dumb with shock. How could she have not known this? How was it that he had kept such a thing secret?

"I'm so sorry," she said, her chest tightening with sympathy for what he had gone through. "You must have been devastated."

"We both were. I was angry at her for dying and I blamed my father for not making her happy when she was alive." He shook his head. "But he blamed himself even more. That's when he began drinking. I think her death haunted him. He couldn't keep a job and eventually we lost the house. We lost everything. As soon as I could, I quit school so that I could work full time and find us another place to live. Eventually, my dad began to pull himself together and we found a stable in Chatham willing to give him another chance. That's when we moved into the apartment over the drugstore."

"Shane..." She had no words in which to express her sympathy for what he'd been through, but hearing his story explained so much, including his reluctance to become involved with her. "I don't know what to say. I never knew...never guessed."

He smiled stoically. "It was a long time ago."

"What about your grandparents? Do you ever see them?"

He shook his head, and his voice turned almost feral. "I have no relationship with them, and no interest in seeing them."

"Does Mitch know all of this?"

"Yes. Why do you think he tolerated having me around so much? He knew how much I hated living over the drugstore. Even though my old man wasn't around that often, I didn't want to spend any time with him."

"Mitch didn't tolerate you. You were his best friend. You were the brother he never had. And as for your father…you sacrificed everything to take care of him," Holly said in amazement. "No wonder you were angry. You were a child, forced to become the adult."

They were quiet for a moment and although Holly wanted to take Shane in her arms and comfort him, she knew instinctively that he would not welcome such a gesture.

"I'm not like her," she finally ventured. "Your mother, I mean."

Shane twisted his head to consider her. "No, you're not."

"I only meant that I appreciate the lifestyle my parents were able to provide me, but I've never felt entitled to it. I have a job and I can take care of myself. I would never depend on someone else, not even a husband."

Shane gave a huff of humorless laughter. "Trust me, I realize that." Shielding his eyes, he looked at the sky. Clouds had begun to form over the lake and a breeze had kicked up, turning the smooth surface of the water into small whitecaps. Pushing himself to his feet, he extended a hand to her. "C'mon, we should head back. Looks like we might get a storm."

Retrieving her panties from where they had been discarded, Holly quickly slipped them on, watching as Shane picked up his T-shirt and pulled it over his head. They folded the quilt in silence and Holly watched as he shoved it unceremoniously back into the tote bag. He was remote and silent during the short walk back to the dinghy, although he took care to help Holly along the uneven path.

She could scarcely believe this was the same man who, less than an hour earlier, had loved her so thoroughly. She had thought that sharing his story with her would have brought them closer together. Instead, he was distant and withdrawn and Holly struggled to find the right words to bring him back. She watched as he pushed the dinghy out onto the water and then pulled strongly on the oars, propelling them swiftly across the choppy water.

By the time they reached the dock, the sky was dark and the water churned beneath them. Shane secured the small boat and, despite the cast on his leg, climbed neatly onto the pier. Holly handed him the cooler and the tote bag, but was unprepared when he reached down and lifted her bodily out of the row boat and onto the dock.

She swayed against him for a moment, her hands braced on his muscular arms. "Are you okay?" she finally asked. "You're so quiet. I didn't mean to dredge up bad memories for you."

The wind ruffled her hair and he pushed a strand of it back from her face. "You didn't," he assured her, but his hazel eyes were turbulent. "The memories are there whether I want them, or not."

A large splotch of water landed on Holly's bare shoulder, followed by another and then another. They both blinked as a sudden flash of lightening streaked overhead, followed by a deafening clap of thunder. Then the skies opened up and a deluge of rain poured down on them.

Shane shoved the tote bag into her hands and turned her around. "Go up to the house," he ordered. "I'll be in as soon as I'm finished here."

"What are you going to do?"

The pelting rain sluiced down his face and plastered his T-shirt against his skin until it was nearly transparent, clinging to his pecs and the layers of muscle on his abdomen. His eyelashes were spiky with moisture. "I'm just going to bring the dinghy into the boathouse. Go on in. You're soaking wet."

His gaze dropped to her breasts and looking down, Holly realized her wet dress clung to her skin, leaving little to the imagination. "What about your cast? Are you sure it's okay to get it wet?"

"It'll be fine!" he shouted as another thunderclap sounded overhead, making her jump. "Now go inside!"

"I can wait for you in the boathouse!" Holly replied, and turned toward the small building.

But Shane captured her wrist in his hand, halting her. "Go up to the main house, Holly. This storm is only going to get worse and I really don't want you in the boathouse. Not after what happened this morning." Another crack of thunder split the sky and Shane turned her toward the house. "Go!"

Holly did. She ran the length of the dock, shielding her eyes against the driving rain, and taking care not to slip on the wet grass as she made her way up the sloping lawn toward the house. She'd just reached the staircase to the deck when a slick patch of ground caused her to lose her balance and stumble forward, and she landed on her knees on the sodden ground. At the same instant another crack of thunder rent the air, and the corner of the top step exploded in a burst of wooden splinters. Time itself seemed to slow down as Holly stared, stupefied, at the damaged step. Slowly, she rose to her feet, but was immediately propelled back to the ground by two hundred pounds of hard, wet male.

"Get down, get down!" Shane shouted, and he covered her body with his own, driving the breath out of her lungs as he flattened her against the wet grass.

She barely had time to register his weight before it was gone. He rolled off of her and jerked her roughly to her feet, half carrying and half dragging her into the shadows beneath the deck where a half dozen kayaks were stacked on a wooden storage rack. Even then, he kept her pressed between his body and the concrete foundation of the house.

"Are you hurt?" he asked urgently, his hands sweeping over her, searching for injuries.

Even in the deep gloom, Holly saw he was white around the mouth and there was a desperation to his touch.

"I'm okay," Holly assured him, gasping for breath as she shivered against him. "What was that?"

"Gunshot," Shane said grimly, peering out at the woods that surrounded the house, as if he might spot the shooter through the battering storm and the protective trees.

"What?" Holly was certain she'd misheard him. "Did you say *gunshot?*"

He turned to look at her, his eyes blazing. "Someone tried to fricking *shoot* you! C'mon, we've got to get into the house and call the police."

Holly followed Shane around the corner of the house to the basement entrance and once they were inside, Shane bolted the door behind them. "Stay right behind me," he ordered quietly. "No lights, no talking. Got it?"

Holly nodded, aware that she was trembling. As she followed him through the basement level and up the stairs to the main house, she hooked her fingers through the belt loops on the back of his shorts, needing to have some contact with him.

When they reached the kitchen, Shane pushed Holly into a sitting position against an interior wall. "Stay here, don't move."

"Be careful." She watched as he made his way quietly through the house, checking to ensure the doors and windows were secure, and surveying the surrounding landscape for any signs of movement. After several long moments he came back, and Holly saw he carried a handgun, which he tucked into the back of his shorts.

"Where did you get that?" she asked, frightened. She'd had weapons training, but until the attack in Iraq, she'd never actually had to use one. Seeing the gun in Shane's hands brought the memories of that day rushing back and she found herself going hot and cold with dread.

"Your dad keeps several guns in a closet upstairs,"

Shane reminded her. He crouched beside her and withdrew his cell phone and then paused to look at her. "Are you sure you're okay?"

"Yes. How did you get to me so quickly back there? I didn't even realize what had happened until you'd pulled me under the deck. And your leg...how did you move so fast?"

"I was watching you go to the house, and then something in the woods distracted me—a movement in the trees. I thought it was a deer and then I heard the gunshot. I saw you fall, and for a second I thought—" He broke off abruptly and swiped a hand over his face. "Christ, Holly."

"I'm okay." Holly rubbed her hands briskly over his arms. "But you need to get out of these wet clothes, Shane. You'll catch cold."

Lowering his hand, Shane looked at her in disbelief and then started to laugh. "You nearly got your head blown off, and you're worried about me catching a cold?"

"Maybe it was a hunter," she suggested hopefully, ignoring his grim humor. "We get hunters in the woods out here sometimes. The lake house is pretty isolated, and sometimes they don't see the marked signs."

Shane pulled out his cell phone and began to punch in numbers, even as he gave her a tolerant look. "Why would a hunter be out in this storm, and what would he be doing so close to the house? He was at the edge of the woods, close enough to realize he was on private property. Even with the rain, no one could have mistaken you for a deer. Not to mention that deer hunting season doesn't begin for another five months."

Holly waited while he made the call, knowing he was

right. But she couldn't think of one reason why anyone would want to shoot at her. The whole incident had to be a mistake; some kind of misunderstanding.

What other explanation could there be?

8

TWO PATROL CARS RESPONDED to Shane's call. One of the officers stayed at the house with Holly, while Shane showed the sheriff and two other deputies where he had seen the movement in the trees. He hadn't wanted to leave Holly in the house, not even with a deputy to protect her. Just thinking about the close call she'd had made him go hot, then cold inside. He replayed the incident in his mind, over and over and each time he felt weak with the realization that she'd nearly been killed. He didn't want to let her out of his sight, even for a second. But he needed to show the sheriff where he'd seen the shooter. There, in the damp pine needles and mud, they retrieved a single shell casing.

"Looks like he left a trail," the sheriff said, crouching down to examine the broken undergrowth. He glanced pointedly at Shane's cast. "Why don't you stay here, while we see what we can find?"

Shane waited while the officers disappeared into the forest. They were gone less than an hour.

"The forest provided some protection from the rain, and we tracked the intruder's path to a dirt road on the edge of the Durant property," the sheriff said. There they'd found some tire marks in the mud, as if someone had left in a hurry, but the rain had turned the entire area into a quagmire and they hadn't been able to obtain any additional evidence.

Except for the bullet.

Outside the house, Shane watched as they dug the spent slug out of the wooden step and examined it.

"The casing looks like a .270 Winchester, and this type of bullet is used fairly commonly among hunters, usually to bring down big game," the sheriff commented, turning the flattened bullet over in his fingers. "Probably fired from a long range hunting rifle, like a Remington 7400."

Shane could see Holly standing just inside the French doors of the kitchen, watching them. He felt restless and irritable. He wanted to hurt someone. He wanted the son of a bitch who had fired that shot behind bars. He wanted to know why he'd taken a crack at Holly. Most of all, he wanted to be in the kitchen with Holly, reassuring her that nothing would happen to her, not while he was there to watch over her. He wanted to know that Holly was safe.

He kept his voice low. "You must have access to the gun permits in this region. Can't you do a cross-check to see who owns one of these hunting rifles?"

The sheriff gave Shane a look of disbelief. "Son, this is Virginia. Every other man in this state owns a hunting rifle. Trying to identify the owner of this particular shell amounts to looking for a needle in a haystack."

"But you don't really think this was some random hunter who thought Holly was a deer, do you?" Shane asked. "Especially considering how the boat engine was rigged. And it's not hunting season."

"Could be just a poacher or vandals. Then again, maybe not." The sheriff narrowed his eyes at Shane. "Maybe it's a disgruntled ex who didn't like seeing her shacked up with you."

"She has no ex, disgruntled or otherwise," Shane bit out.

"Maybe it's someone who has a grudge against her daddy, or has something against the war. Hell, boy, we could stand here all night exchanging discourse on the vagaries of human nature, but until we get this bullet back to a forensics lab, we're not going to know much."

Shane scrubbed a hand across his hair, frustrated. "Okay, fine. But let me know as soon as you learn anything."

"You might want to bring Ms. Durant back to her parents' house in Chatham," the sheriff suggested. "At least until we get this thing figured out. Be a damn shame to have her survive getting gunshot in Iraq, only to get killed in her own summer home. She'll be safer in Chatham, where it's not so remote."

Shane bristled at the implication, despite knowing the sheriff was right. "She'll be safe here, with me. And I'd appreciate it if you didn't mention this to her parents. At least not until we know for sure what happened. They're worried enough about her as it is."

"Right." The officer's expression didn't change, but his tone suggested he didn't agree with Shane, either about keeping Holly safe or about keeping her parents ignorant of the afternoon's events.

Shane watched them leave and returned to the house,

closing the door with a decisive click, before throwing the deadbolt. They were a bunch of idiots; keystone cops who probably spent more time in the local donut shop than they did actually fighting crime. He had absolutely no confidence that they would trace the bullet back to a weapon, or the weapon back to an actual person.

He couldn't imagine why anyone would want to harm Holly, but the officer's words haunted him. Did Holly have a former boyfriend who might have seen them on the island together and been angry enough to want to kill her? Shane was certain that if she hadn't slipped on the wet grass, the bullet would have struck her in the skull.

The thought made him go queasy and he bent his head to the doorframe as he sucked in air and reminded himself that she was okay. Nothing was going to happen to her while he was there. He wouldn't allow it.

"Hey, are you okay?"

He pushed himself away from the wall and straightened, giving Holly what he hoped was a reassuring smile. "Yeah, I'm good. How about you?"

"I'm fine. What did they say? Was it a hunter?"

Shane looked sharply at her. She didn't actually believe the shooting had been an accident, did she? Her expression was both hopeful and frightened, and he realized that he didn't want to tell her about his suspicions. She'd been through too much. How much more could she take? In that instant, she seemed both vulnerable and fragile to him, but he wouldn't lie to her.

"A poacher, most likely," he conceded. "With the heavy rain, he probably mistook you for a deer, or maybe the storm startled him into firing accidentally. Either way, there's no sign of him now."

"What a relief." A light shudder ran through her. "I'm so glad you're here. I love the lake house but sometimes it seems very isolated."

"Who knows you're out here?"

Holly shrugged. "My parents. My friend, Susan, who drove me here. Pete Larson. I think that's it. I was trying to get away from people, so to tell everyone that I was coming to the lake house would have defeated my purpose."

"Do you have any former boyfriends or lovers who might object to you being here with me?" He said the words brusquely, trying to keep his voice matter-of-fact. She was entitled to a past that didn't involve him.

"What?" Her voice registered her astonishment. "You don't actually believe this was anything more than an accident, do you? I've been coming out here my entire life and nothing like this has ever happened before."

"My point, exactly. So why now, when you're here with me?"

"The very idea is ludicrous!"

"Holly, just tell me," he persisted, feeling like a Class A jerk. Now she was completely freaked out, but there was no turning back. "Is there someone who might be jealous or angry enough to want to hurt you? Or scare you?"

"No!" She gestured wildly with one hand. "As pathetic as it sounds, there isn't a single guy I can think of who would care if I slept with an entire platoon of Marines, never mind just one."

I would care.

For a heart-stopping moment, Shane thought he might have uttered the words aloud, but when Holly's expression didn't change, he relaxed just a little. He hadn't expected her to have hordes of former lovers. But neither had he expected her to remain celibate during the past three years. It only made sense that a girl with Holly's looks and personality would have had at least a few former boyfriends.

"What about you?" she asked archly. "No jealous girlfriends out there who might want me out of the picture?"

Her tone was light, but Shane didn't miss how she waited for his response. He gave her a look. "Hardly. You're probably the only woman alive who hasn't figured out that I'm not a great catch. Like I already told you, I'm a realist, not a romantic. Most women prefer the latter."

Shane hadn't been a saint since he joined the military, but his few relationships had been casual and short-lived. He wasn't the kind of guy to make promises to a woman, not when he spent so much time deployed. That had been part of the reason he'd left the morning after Holly's graduation party without so much as a thank-you or a good-bye. If he'd hung around long enough for her to wake up in his arms, he would have insisted that she wait for him, even knowing they couldn't have any kind of relationship while they were both in the military. The knowledge had scared him enough that he'd gotten the hell out of there before he'd done something completely insane.

Like leave the Marine Corps.

Or ask her to marry him.

"Call me crazy, then," Holly said, watching him. "I happen to think you're a great catch."

Shane wanted to drag her into his arms and cover her mouth with his own; anything to shut her up, because when she looked at him like that, all soft and sexy, it took all the restraint he had not to confess how he really felt.

"I'm going to check the perimeter of the house," he said abruptly. "Turn the security system on while I'm gone."

She looked at him, puzzled. "How long will you be?"

"An hour, no more."

"To do a walk-around of the property?" Her voice expressed her disbelief.

"I need to think, and I can't do it in here," he finally said. "The fresh air will help clear my head. I have a key, so if you want to go upstairs, that's probably not a bad idea."

To his relief, she accepted his explanation. Once outside, he paused and cocked his head to listen, but except for the night bugs in the trees, everything was silent. He was convinced that whoever had taken the shot at Holly had intended to hurt or kill her. This had been no accident.

There was a part of him that wondered if he shouldn't bring her back to her parents' house in Chatham, as the police had suggested. Maybe she would be safer there. But in the next instant, he realized that wasn't an option. If someone was intent on harming Holly, then returning to Chatham could put her parents in danger, too. Until the culprit was captured, he wasn't leaving her side. He'd let her down once; he wouldn't do it again.

HOLLY STOOD AT THE WINDOW for a moment and watched as Shane walked down the gravel driveway, his gait slightly uneven due to his cast. After a moment, the shadows swallowed him up, and as much as she strained to peer through the darkness, she could no longer detect him.

The afternoon's events had shaken her more than she cared to admit. She didn't want Shane to leave the house; wanted him to stay inside with her, where it was safe. If there was some crazed gunman out there, she didn't want Shane in danger. But she'd known that to argue with him would have been pointless. She had some comfort knowing that he had her father's handgun with him, and that he knew how to use it.

Walking back into the great room, she took one look at the towering wall of windows overlooking the water and realized she couldn't remain there. She could almost feel malevolent eyes watching her from the trees beyond the house. If there actually was someone out there with a gun, she'd be an easy target in the brightly lit room.

The small clock in the front hallway chimed, and Holly nearly leaped out of her skin.

"Okay, that's it," she muttered under her breath. "I'm outta here."

Darting up the stairs, she made her way to her bedroom and pulled the drapes tightly closed across her windows before switching on the bedside lamp. It was just after eight o'clock, and there was no way she was going to be able to sleep, not with Shane wandering around outside. Restless and agitated, she prowled the room. She felt helpless, and she didn't like it one bit. She wanted to be with Shane. She knew how to handle a weapon, but with her injured arm, she'd be more of a liability to him than an asset.

She heard the back door open and then close, and Shane's distinct footsteps as he crossed the first floor.

He came up the stairs and when he appeared in the doorway of Holly's bedroom, it was all she could do not to launch herself at him.

"Anything?" she asked.

He shook his head. "No. Everything looks normal. I locked the boathouse and turned on the security system." He hesitated. "If you're too nervous to stay here, I'll understand. I can use the Jeep to drive you back to Chatham, or we could stay in a hotel somewhere."

"No!" Holly felt her heartbeat accelerate. She didn't want to leave Shane; didn't want to be separated from him for any reason, not even to allow him to go out to the barn and start the Jeep. A part of her worried that if she let him out of her sight now, she would never see him again. "I'm not afraid to stay here, as long as you're with me. And the sheriff promised to make extra patrols along the lake road tonight, just to be safe."

Shane turned away, but not before Holly saw the flash of relief in his hazel eyes. With a sense of shock, she realized that he didn't want her to leave any more than she wanted to go. She watched as he withdrew the handgun from the back of his waistband and placed it on the bedside table.

"I don't think whoever fired that shot is going to return, but it doesn't hurt to take precautions." He moved to the window and flicked the edge of her curtain aside, peering out at the dark yard.

Holly sat down on the edge of the bed and scrubbed her hands over her face. "I can't believe it happened. Who would want to hurt either of us?"

Turning away from the window, Shane came and sat down next to her. "If not personal, then what about someone in your professional life? Can you think of any reason why someone from your battalion might want to hurt you?"

Holly lowered her hands and stared at him, bewildered. "My entire unit is still in Iraq. None of them even know where I live, never mind that I'm here at the lake house."

Shane blew out a hard breath. "You're right. I'm just trying to cover all the angles."

"And what if I'm not the target? What if you are?"

"I've considered that, but I'm coming up blank. I can't think of a single reason why anyone would want to kill me. Plus, this is *your* family's house."

Holly shuddered. "God, this is so creepy."

"We can still leave."

The thought of Shane walking out to the barn where the family kept the Jeep unnerved her. Even if he succeeded in getting the vehicle running, they still had a mile of dark, isolated road to traverse before they would reach the main road and anything resembling civilization. They would be an easy target for someone who might be lurking in the nearby woods.

"I think we should stay here tonight. We can make a final decision in the morning," she finally answered.

Shane glanced at the bedside clock. "It's been a long day, and you didn't get much sleep last night. Why don't you turn in?"

"What about you?" She had hoped that he would stay with her. She wanted to feel his solid presence beside her, to know that he was safe and would keep her safe.

He rose to his feet and indicated the overstuffed chair in one corner of her room. "I'll be right here."

"You can't sleep in that chair, Shane," she protested.

He was still recovering from his injuries. He needed sleep as much as she did, but knowing he was so close would ensure she'd be awake the entire night.

"I don't intend to sleep. I intend to watch over you."

9

HOLLY AWOKE WITH A start to find Shane bending over her, his fingers pressed lightly against her lips. Despite her efforts, she had fallen asleep and now the bedroom was so dark she could barely make out his features.

"Shh," he breathed in her ear. "There's somebody in the house."

Panic swamped her and she tried to sit up, struggling against Shane's restraining hands.

"Listen to me." His voice was hushed, but there was no denying the authority in it. "I want you to go into the bathroom, very quietly, and stay there until I tell you that you can come out."

He removed his fingers and pulled back the sheet, urging her to her feet. Holly felt him press something cold and hard into her hands. "Take this, and if the intruder gets past me, use it."

Holly curled the fingers of her good hand around the gun, testing its weight. "What about you?" she whispered.

"I can take care of myself *and* the bastard downstairs," he hissed. "C'mon. Very quietly, now."

Holly let him guide her across the bedroom and into the adjoining bathroom, where he pushed her against the wall beside the door. There was a night-light on over the sink and by the dim glow, she could see Shane's face, all sharp angles and dark shadows. From somewhere in the house below them, Holly heard a noise. As noises went, it wasn't much, no more than a soft footfall, but the very furtiveness of it caused the short hairs on the back of her neck to stand up. Her eyes flew to Shane's.

"No matter what happens, or what you hear," he whispered, "do not leave this position until I tell you to."

"Be careful," she whispered back, and watched as Shane melded into the gloom of the bedroom. She stood with her back pressed against the wall, holding the gun with two hands as she had been trained to do. She had no desire to use it, but if it meant her life or Shane's, she wouldn't hesitate. Her heart hammered in her chest, but she felt oddly calm. They had the advantage of surprise, and they were armed. There was no question they would prevail.

How had the intruder gotten past the security system? Or maybe he hadn't and even now, the sheriff was on his way out to the lake house. Holly fervently hoped that was case. She desperately wanted to peer around the doorframe and into the bedroom, but she wouldn't do anything that might betray their position or put Shane in danger.

Keeping her breathing shallow, she tensed when she heard a floorboard depress in the hallway outside her bedroom. Her fingers tightened around the pistol and she waited. She was familiar enough with the sounds of the house to know when the bedroom door opened, very slowly. Then all hell broke loose.

SHANE WAITED JUST INSIDE the bedroom, behind the door. He had a gun, but he didn't want to kill the bastard; he wanted him alive. He held his breath as the door to the bedroom swung slowly inward and a dark shape moved stealthily through. Even in the darkness, Shane could see he wasn't a big guy, but he was thick set through the shoulders and chest. He wore a black cap pulled down low over his eyes, and as moonlight filtered through the overhead skylights, he distinctly saw the gun that the other man held in his hand.

Shane waited until the man fully entered the room and then brought his fisted hands, holding the gun butt, down on the back of the man's head. The man grunted but instead of going down, he staggered and then turned, swinging his weapon up. Shane drove his elbow into the man's face and at the same time, used his own weapon to strike the man's wrist. With a pained cry, the other man dropped the gun, but used his body as a battering ram, lunging at Shane and using his momentum to send them both crashing into the nearby dresser.

As Shane struggled to keep his balance, his attacker swung at his face. Shane twisted his head at the last minute, but the man's meaty fist caught him on the temple, causing brilliant sparks to shoot behind his eyes. With an enraged roar, he got the man in a bear hug, ignoring the punishing blows pummeling his sides.

"Stop, or I *will* kill you," came a calm voice, in the same instant that the lights flicked on. "I have a gun, and I will shoot."

Over the attacker's shoulder, Shane saw Holly standing in the open doorway to the bathroom, pointing a handgun at them with both hands. The interruption distracted the intruder, and as he turned to face Holly,

Shane pistol-whipped him across the side of the head and watched with grim satisfaction as he crumpled soundlessly to the floor.

Pushing his weapon into the waistband at the back of his shorts, he didn't wait, but immediately bent over the man and flipped him onto his stomach, pulling his arms behind him.

"Quick, get me something to restrain him," he ordered.

Holly, wide-eyed and pale, jerked open the top drawer of a small dresser and pulled out several pairs of sheer stockings. "Can you use these?"

"Perfect," Shane said, using the filmy material to bind the man's wrists together, before moving to his ankles.

Only when he was satisfied that the intruder couldn't free himself, did he roll him onto his back. He was semi-conscious, his eyes fluttering weakly as he muttered something unintelligible. Shane glanced at Holly, but saw she was already calling the police, speaking quietly into her cell phone as her gaze flicked involuntarily to the man on the floor. She looked shaken.

Reaching down, Shane dragged the hat from the bastard's head, noting with satisfaction the nasty gash over his ear that oozed blood. He guessed the intruder was in his late twenties. He was Hispanic, with dark, curly hair and black eyes and a short, stocky build.

"Who the hell are you and what do you want?" Shane snarled, half-lifting the man from the floor by the front of his shirt.

"Go to hell," the man said weakly, but his dark eyes blazed with fear and resentment.

"Holly, do you recognize this man?"

Holly snapped her cell phone shut and came to stand several feet away as she studied the man's face. "No," she finally said, shaking her head. "I've never seen him before in my life."

Shane dropped the man back against the floorboards and systematically began patting him down and searching his pockets.

"Shouldn't you wait for the sheriff?" Holly asked, watching him.

"This man wanted to kill us," Shane said. "I want to know why, and I want to know now."

Reaching into the man's pockets, he pulled out several folded papers and a set of keys, but no wallet or identification. Unfolding the papers, Shane scanned them quickly and felt his rage grow. Written on the paper was Holly's address in Chatham, and some notes about her recent activities. Beneath that were written directions to the lake house, and a crude diagram of the property, complete with access roads and buildings.

Pulling his gun free from his shorts, Shane thrust the barrel beneath the man's jaw, enjoying how the other guy's eyes popped open in terror. "Tell me who you are and why you're here, or I will kill you right now."

"Shane, no!"

Shane ignored Holly's alarmed protest.

"Tell me," he ground out, his face scant inches from the other man's, "or I'll tell the sheriff you were unfortunately killed during the break-in. Who do you think they're going to believe?"

"Go ahead," the man sneered, his face twisting. "Kill me. But it won't end. There are others like me who will come after her."

Her. As in Holly.

"You son of a bitch," Shane growled, shifting the gun to the base of the man's neck. "Tell me why you're here or I swear, I'll sever your spinal cord and you can live the rest of your life eating, breathing, and pissing through tubes."

"Shane."

Shane's gaze flicked to Holly's, and he saw the deep disquiet in her eyes. He had to draw on every ounce of training and restraint he had not to make good on his promise right then and there. The only thing that stopped him was the expression on Holly's face, and the fact that until he learned what the man's motives were, her life would continue to be in danger.

Reluctantly, he withdrew the pistol from the man's neck and set it on top of the dresser. Rising to his feet, he swiped a hand over his face. He'd never felt so helpless in his entire life as he did at that moment.

"Come here," he said roughly, and extended a hand to Holly. She came to him immediately, wrapping her arms around him and pressing her face against his chest. "I don't want you to worry. This guy is nothing, okay? Nobody is going to hurt you, not while I'm here."

She nodded. "I'm not afraid for myself. Only for you. I thought he was going to kill you."

In the distance, they heard the sound of police sirens drawing closer. "Go downstairs and let them in," Shane advised. "I'll stay here with our guest."

Holly pulled away. "You're not going to hurt him, are you?"

Shane wanted to beat the man bloody, but he shook his head. "I'm not going to touch him." At her doubtful look, he sighed. "I promise, all right?"

He listened to her footsteps recede and heard when

she opened the door to admit the sheriff and his men. His eyes shifted back to the man on the floor.

"I will find out what you're after," he said grimly. "And then I'll make you sorry you were ever born."

IT WAS SEVERAL HOURS before the sheriff left with the intruder, and even after intensive questioning, the man had refused to divulge his name or his reason for breaking in. In fact, he'd been stoically quiet, refusing to provide even the most basic of information. Shane would have been happy to spend the rest of the night interrogating the man the good old-fashioned way, but the sheriff had decided it was time to get him to a hospital and have his head injury treated, after which he would be transferred to the county jail. Shane had pulled the sheriff aside and had repeated what the man had said about there being additional men who would come after Holly if he failed in his mission to kill her.

"Well, he could be bluffing, of course. But if I were you, I would think seriously about returning her to her father's house in Chatham. The sheriff's office there can provide her with the kind of around-the-clock security that she needs until we get this thing straightened out." He'd paused. "I know you think you can keep her safe, but the reality is that this might be bigger than you. She's made some enemies, and if what this man said is true, they're not going to stop until they get rid of her. And anyone who stands in their way."

After they were gone, Holly poured herself a small glass of whiskey and Shane watched with a mixture of amusement and concern as she quaffed it in a single, long swallow.

"I didn't know you drank this stuff," he observed,

accepting the glass she offered to him and tossing it quickly back.

"I don't," she said, shuddering lightly. "But that doesn't mean I can't, when the occasion calls for it. You don't go through the academy without learning how to handle the hard stuff."

Setting the glass aside, Shane drew her carefully into his arms. "Are you okay?"

She tipped her head against his chest. "I've never been so frightened in my whole life. Not even that day in Iraq."

Shane felt his chest tighten. She'd been through too much, and he didn't want to cause her more worry and distress than she was already feeling. As soon as it was light, he'd bring her back to Chatham. Because as much as he hated to admit it, he couldn't keep her safe, and the lake house was too remote for the police to effectively patrol the property.

"It's almost dawn," he murmured against her hair. "We'll head into town tomorrow, but right now you should try to get some rest."

They would need to file a formal statement at the sheriff's office later that morning, but Shane could see that Holly was swaying on her feet with exhaustion. The events of the night had taken a toll on her, both physically and emotionally.

"I don't think I can sleep," she protested. "What if another of his henchmen comes? If this guy got through the security system, what's to say another one won't?"

"Because there are two deputies on the property right now. One at the front of the house and one at the back. They won't leave and nobody is going to disturb us."

She shivered in his arms and then yawned hugely. "Okay, but just for a few hours."

Shane steered her toward the stairs, determined that after they visited the sheriff's office, he would insist that she return to her father's house in Chatham. The sheriff had been correct. It would be easier to protect her there than it would be at the lake house.

At the doorway to her bedroom, Shane stopped. Every cell in his body urged him to stay with her, but after what she had been through, she needed rest more than she needed him.

Holly paused and turned to Shane with a questioning look. He took a step back, when all he really wanted to do was to haul her against his body and never let her go.

"Shane." Her voice was so soft and low that he had to bend his head to catch her words. "Don't leave me tonight."

"Holly…"

"I need you, Shane. I swear, I won't sleep a wink unless you stay with me. I'll jump at every noise and shadow. Please."

He looked into her dark eyes and knew he couldn't resist her pleading. But he wouldn't take advantage of her vulnerability. He could stay in her room without sleeping in her bed.

"Okay," he relented. "But I'll stay in the chair."

To his surprise, she capitulated. "Okay. Just don't—" she yawned "—leave me."

"I won't."

Shane realized it was the truth. If he had his way, he'd never leave her again. But even if he was the kind of guy who could give her what she needed—which he wasn't—there was still the issue of their disparate ranks. If the brass knew just how friendly they had become, he and Holly could face formal charges. He might lose a few stripes, but Holly's career would be permanently ruined. Shane knew Holly well enough to guess that she might consider herself too damaged to return to active duty, but he'd seen soldiers who had lost legs and arms return to service. She was intelligent and hard-working and the Navy would be fortunate to have her. Eventually, she'd come to the same realization. He didn't want her to throw a promising future down the toilet because of him.

If he was smart, he'd haul her ass back to Chatham right that minute and leave her on daddy's doorstep, while he high-tailed it back to Camp Lejeune.

But he wasn't smart.

He was a complete dumb-ass, because he fully intended to stay the night in Holly's room. And then he intended to give her the three weeks she had asked for.

10

SHANE LOUNGED IN THE chair with his foot up on a small stool while Holly slept. She'd come out of the bathroom about an hour earlier wearing a T-shirt and a pair of shorts and had climbed into bed with a blissful sigh of relief. She'd patted the mattress beside her, insisting that Shane could at least recline on top of the blanket while he kept vigil, but Shane had refused. He didn't trust himself to be in the same bed with Holly. He'd be fine as long as he was awake, but if he fell asleep, he'd be drawn to her feminine warmth and scent like a magnet.

Despite the discomfort of the chair and his own determination not to fall asleep, Shane found his eyelids drifting closed, but he snapped to full awareness when Holly made a small sound of distress. Sitting up, he strained to see her through the indistinct light. She lay on her side, but she shifted restlessly against the sheets. She was dreaming, and as Shane wondered whether or not to wake her, she made a moaning sound of anguish. He lowered his foot to the floor and leaned forward. She turned her face into the pillow and Shane could see her fists bunching in the flowered fabric.

"No, please," she whimpered, and her voice was so small and un-Holly-like, that Shane's chest tightened.

Debating only a moment, he eased himself onto the mattress beside her and carefully gathered her against his chest. She resisted for a fraction of a second, until he murmured soothingly to her.

"Shane," she breathed, and relaxed against him. "I had a terrible dream…"

"Shh," he soothed. "Go to sleep. I'm here." He lay back on the pillows with her face cushioned on his shoulder and her body soft and lax against his. She drew in a shuddering sigh and murmured something unintelligible.

"Everything's okay," he murmured. "Go back to sleep."

She burrowed closer, and he waited as her breathing deepened. After several moments, she gave a soft snore. Her silky hair tickled his jaw, and her warm breath fanned his neck. The pressure of her breasts against his side was torture, so he concentrated instead on the small, illuminated clock on the bedside table, watching as the minutes clicked by and wondering how in hell he would make it through the rest of the night.

He had only to turn his head to inhale her fragrance, and when she shifted closer and drew a leg up and over his thigh, he almost groaned in despair. Despite his resolve not to touch her in anything other than a platonic fashion, he was rock hard for her.

He drew in several deep breaths and willed his body to relax. The events of the day had left him completely jacked, but he didn't need physical release as much as he needed to just hold Holly and reassure himself that she was safe. He tightened his arm around her, and eventually drifted into sleep with the sweet weight of her body pinning him to the bed.

HOLLY DIDN'T KNOW how long she'd slept; she was only aware of the long, hard length of fully aroused male pressed against her backside. Her head was pillowed on Shane's bicep and his other arm was flung across her body. Beneath the sheet, her bare legs were tangled with his, and his cast was hard and scratchy against her skin. She could tell by his breathing that he was still asleep, and she shifted experimentally against him. He muttered something incoherent and his hand curved possessively around her breast.

She knew the instant he came awake and realized just where he was, and sensed from the instant coiling of his muscles that he intended to pull away. Before he could move, she covered his hand with her own, pushing her breast into his palm.

He stopped breathing.

Smiling, Holly arched her back and rubbed her bottom sensuously against his erection. He groaned on an exhale of breath and his hand began to caress her breast, fondling and plucking at the nipple beneath her shirt. Holly stroked the length of his good leg with her foot, reveling in the light furring of hair and the hard muscles of his calf.

"Mmm," she sighed, pulling his hand to her other breast, "that feels so good."

He nuzzled the nape of her neck and then caught her earlobe with his teeth, biting gently before soothing the area with his tongue. Holly shivered in pleasure.

"Do you like that?" His voice was rough with sleep and arousal.

In answer, Holly pushed his hand down to the hem of her T-shirt and then helped him to drag it upward, exposing her breasts to the cool air and his warm hand.

"Touch me," she murmured.

With a small noise of defeat, Shane rose over her and captured her mouth in a kiss that she felt all the way to her toes. At the same time, he covered her bare breast in one big hand. She could feel the hard calluses on his palm, the rough whiskers on his jaw, and she reveled in the sheer masculinity of him. She kissed him back, stroking her tongue against his as she tunneled her fingers through his hair, enjoying the velvety texture of the short strands.

Shane broke the kiss first to dip his head and kiss her breast, flicking her nipple with his tongue until he drew it into his mouth, suckling her hard. Holly gasped as the insistent pull of his hot mouth caused an answering throb of arousal deep in her sex. She curled her legs around his and reached down to cover him with her hand. Even through the fabric of his shorts, she could feel his heat and ached to have him inside her.

"Take these off," she whispered, caressing the back of his head with her other hand.

Reaching down, Shane pushed her hand away and with one flick, unfastened his shorts, pushing them down over his hips as Holly used her feet to push them completely free. And then there he was, throbbing and hot against her stomach. She took him in her hand and stroked her thumb along the sensitive underside, before smoothing her finger over the blunt cap. He gave a low growl of pleasure and released her breast to slowly work his way down her body, planting moist kisses along her ribcage and stomach, until he reached the waistband of her shorts. Without pausing, he undid the snap and swept both the shorts and her underwear down over her hips in one smooth movement until she was naked beneath him.

"Oh man," Shane breathed, using his hands to push her thighs apart, "you really are gorgeous down here, all pink and pillowy-soft."

In answer, Holly slid her hand over her stomach and through the small cluster of curls to where she ached for him. She parted her folds, watching Shane as he watched her. His expression was one of rapture, and she felt herself pulse hotly in response. But when she would have swirled her fingers over her clitoris, he grasped her wrist and pinned it to her side.

"Oh, no," he rasped, "that's my job." And he bent his head and swept his tongue over her, causing her to cry out in startled pleasure. He licked her relentlessly, lapping at her until she gave a strangled moan and pushed helplessly at his shoulders.

"Stop," she panted. "I can't take any more."

In answer, Shane released her, reaching over, he opened the bedside drawer and withdrew a small packet from the stash of condoms she'd appropriated from Mitch's room. Covering himself, he came up to lay alongside her. He ran his hand almost reverently over her breasts and stomach, and Holly knew her entire body was flushed from his lovemaking. She thought he would come over her, settle himself between her thighs and finally ease the relentless aching need, but he didn't.

Lying on his side, he pulled her close and then raised her leg and bent her knee back. She felt him, heavy and hot, at her opening, and she shifted to grant him better access. Slowly, with his gaze fixed on her, he began to ease himself into her, stretching her and filling her. The angle of his penetration caused her mouth to open in wordless surprise, and when he began to slowly thrust, she clutched his arm and lifted herself mindlessly into the intense pleasure.

Shane hooked her knee over his arm and opened her wider, his movements growing stronger. Holly watched in wonder as his face grew taut and his breathing changed, and still he studied her, as if he was attuned to everything she felt. His eyes glowed faintly green in the pale sunlight that filtered through the skylights.

"Good?" he asked, his voice husky with strain.

"Oh, yeah… So good…"

As if to disprove her words and show her that it could be better still, Shane gave a subtle rotation of his hips as he thrust. Holly gasped, her inner muscles clenching greedily at the pleasure he provided, feeling her orgasm building and gathering in on itself. She was so close, but she didn't want to let go yet, not when Shane was watching her with an expression that made her heart stop, and then explode into a frenzied rhythm in her chest. But when he let out a low groan and thrust deeply, the cords in his neck standing out, Holly couldn't hold back any longer and convulsed around him, splintering into a billion glittering bits, following him into the vortex of pleasure.

As Holly struggled to control her ragged breathing, she realized one truth; whatever she thought she'd felt for Shane before was nothing compared to how she felt about him now. She wanted to stay with him like this forever. She wanted to bottle the moment and tuck it into her pocket.

Withdrawing carefully from her, Shane pulled her against his chest and kissed her with a sweetness that made tears prick behind her eyelids. Pulling away, he gazed down at her as if he would memorize each feature.

"Holly…" He swallowed hard. "I just want you to know that I—"

From downstairs there came the sound of someone knocking on the front door of the house.

Shane swore softly and then gave a huff of laughter. "My timing sucks."

"I don't think so," Holly responded, pressing her lips against his shoulder. "After all, whoever is knocking could have showed up ten minutes ago. Now that would have been bad timing. What were you going to say?"

The knocking came again, more insistent this time. With a groan of frustration, Shane pulled away.

"Nothing." But when Holly would have sat up, Shane forestalled her. "I'll get the door. You stay."

Holly tamped down her own frustration and rolled onto her stomach as she watched Shane clean up and then hunt for his discarded clothing. What had he been going to say? Holly, I want you to know…what? That he loved her? That he didn't love her? The not knowing would drive her nuts.

Shane glanced at the bedside clock. "Christ, I didn't realize how late it is. That's probably the sheriff downstairs."

Holly grimaced. "I'm almost afraid to hear what he

has to say about our unwelcome visitor. I'm just going to take a quick shower and get dressed, and then I'll be right down."

HOLLY HEARD THE LOW murmur of masculine voices coming from the Great Room as she descended the stairs. She took a deep breath and told herself she was prepared for whatever the sheriff might tell her about the intruder. But nothing could have prepared her for the sight of two uniformed Navy officers sitting on the leather sofa. Her gaze flew to Shane, who stood by the massive fireplace wearing nothing but a pair of shorts and a rumpled T-shirt. Next to the spit-polish shine of the two officers, Holly could only guess how uncomfortable he must feel. In the same instant, she noticed the glossy binder that lay on the coffee table between the two sofas. Even from where she stood, she recognized the insignia of the office of the Naval Inspector General.

She froze and for the space of a heartbeat, she couldn't breathe, couldn't think. The only thing that flashed through her mind was that she had just ruined Shane's military career.

Someone knew about the two of them and had reported them! The sole mission of the Inspector General was to investigate allegations of inappropriate behavior, including unethical relationships between officers and enlisted members. And the kicker was, even if she told the investigators that she was completely in love with Shane and intended to leave the military, it wouldn't matter. None of that would matter. Shane would still be punished. But who could have reported them?

Panicked, Holly tried to think. Nobody in her unit

knew anything about her relationship with Shane, and since they'd returned to the States, she was pretty sure that Pete Larson was the only person who might have guessed they were more than just old friends—but he would have nothing to gain by reporting them. None of it made any sense.

Holly hesitated, ready to creep back to the second floor, but it was too late. The two officers had seen her and were rising to their feet, hats in hand, watching as she stood motionless. Behind them, Shane made a helpless gesture of resignation.

Drawing a deep breath, Holly smoothed her hands over the front of her sleeveless top and slowly made her way down to where the men stood, acutely conscious of her bare feet and wet hair. She knew how damning the situation looked.

"Lieutenant Durant," said the first officer, stepping forward to extend his hand. "I'm Lieutenant Commander Fowler and this is Lieutenant Harrington. Pardon us for disturbing you during your, ah, recuperation, but your father told us you were out here."

Holly couldn't help herself; her eyes flashed to Shane's. She saw the warning in them and the subtle shake of his head, but there was no way she was letting him take the hit for anything. After all, she'd pretty much begged him to sleep with her. Drawing a deep breath, she turned to Fowler.

"I just want you to know that Sgt. Rafferty had nothing to do with this. I—I pulled rank to coerce him into sleeping with me, and he felt he had no choice but to go along with it."

Lt. Fowler exchanged meaningful glances with his

partner, but before he could respond, Shane stepped forward.

"Holly, stop." His voice was low and urgent. "They're here about Sgt. Martinez."

For a moment, Holly had absolutely no idea who he was talking about. Then she recalled the sad-eyed supply clerk who had been riding in the supply truck with her on the day of the incident. Her mouth opened on a wordless 'o' of realization, and her face turned hot with embarrassment. At the same time, a tidal wave of relief washed over her, making her feel weak. This wasn't about her involvement with Shane, although she'd certainly given the investigators sufficient cause to probe further into their relationship. She glanced at Shane, but he kept his gaze fixed resolutely on the opposite wall.

Struggling to maintain her composure, she sat down in a chair adjacent to the sofa. "What about Sgt. Martinez?"

Lt. Harrington leaned forward and opened the binder. Holly saw it was a dossier of sorts, with a uniformed photo of Sgt. Martinez, and an assortment of official looking documents and transcripts. He turned the binder so that Holly could look at it.

"Do you know this man?"

"Yes, that's Sgt. Martinez." Holly shifted her gaze between the two men. "Is this about the missing supplies and equipment?"

LCDR Fowler nodded. "That's right. Before you were injured, you reported that you suspected Sgt. Martinez might be involved in stealing government property."

Holly nodded. "Yes. I was in charge of all the supply operations for the Seabees in Iraq. Al Asad was the largest supply depot, but not the only one that I oversaw.

When I arrived at the air base, one of the first things I did was to perform an inventory of what we had on hand, and to reconcile that with the hand-receipts for what we had received and distributed." She paused, trying to recall the details of what she had found. "There were a lot of inconsistencies and missing receipts, and when I did a funding reconciliation, there was over a hundred thousand dollars that I couldn't account for."

Lt. Harrington leaned forward. "Sgt. Martinez was the supply clerk in charge of maintaining both the records and the funding. Did you speak to him about your findings?"

"Of course. He seemed to have a hundred different excuses for why he hadn't obtained the required documentation for the equipment that was missing. Initially, they seemed like valid reasons but the more I dug into the paperwork, the more questions I had. When I asked Sgt. Martinez about the funding, he insisted there must have been an input error that had resulted in the discrepancy." Holly paused. "I suspected something unethical was going on, but I couldn't be sure. I thought that maybe he was skimming money from the funding pool, or working deals with the local contractors, but I just didn't have the background or expertise to know for sure."

"So you had him moved to Camp Fallujah."

"That's right. There's a senior supply officer there whom I trust, and since he doesn't maintain a huge inventory or a large cash fund, I believed Sgt. Martinez would be in a position to do less harm."

"Based on your allegations," said Lt. Harrington, "we initiated an investigation into his actions while in the supply position at Al Asad. We have reason to believe that during the eighteen months of his service on that base, he diverted more than one million dollars to various accounts, both here in the States, and offshore."

Holly gasped. "What? How is that even possible? I mean, I know he had access to a supply fund, but one million dollars? That's just not possible."

"That's just the tip of the iceberg," LCDR Fowler said. "Not only did he have access to the supply funds in order to procure goods in-country, but he also had the authority to award contracts for other assets."

"Has he been arrested?"

Lt. Harrington shook his head. "Not yet. He's not even aware he's the subject of an active investigation, nor will he be until we have enough evidence to indict him. We need to know the extent of the scheme, and who else might be involved before we make an arrest."

Holly frowned. "I don't understand how he's benefitting from the contracts he oversees. I know that he oversaw a contract for bottled water. How is that lucrative?"

"We suspect that Sgt. Martinez steered a fifteen million dollar contract for bottled water to Haley LLC, and received over five hundred thousand dollars in payment for his actions."

Holly pressed her fingers against her eyes. "Oh my God. I had no idea." Lowering her hands, she looked at the two officers. "No offense, but Sgt. Martinez never struck me as being the brightest bulb on the tree. He had to have help. I just can't believe he was capable of doing this on his own. For one thing, he didn't have that kind of authority." Holly gave a disbelieving laugh. "Even I didn't have that kind of authority. Our procurements were limited to simple acquisitions."

"We believe he and several contracting officers working in Iraq had an extensive network of contractors that they did business with. Questionable business."

"Have you questioned any of them?" Holly asked, but her attention was momentarily distracted as Shane bent over the coffee table and swiveled the binder around so that he could better see the photo of Sgt. Martinez. His expression was troubled. "What is it, Shane?"

He frowned and scrubbed a hand across the back of his neck. "I don't know. It's probably nothing."

LCDR Fowler turned toward Shane. "Do you know something about this individual?"

Shane shook his head. "I'm not sure. He looks familiar to me, but…no. I don't know him."

"What do you need from me?" Holly asked, drawing the officer's attention from Shane.

"We want you to tell us everything you remember about your interactions with Sgt. Martinez and the supply operations. What made you suspicious, what the records showed, et cetera. We'll need a full statement from you."

Holly glanced at Shane. "This might take awhile."

He nodded brusquely. "Right. I'll be in the garage. I have a couple of projects I'm working on, and I want to take a look at the Jeep."

Holly waited until Shane had left the house and then turned to the other two officers. LCDR Fowler arched a questioning eyebrow.

"He's my brother's best friend," she finally said, but couldn't prevent the heat that washed into her face. "We've known each other since we were kids."

"How long have you been involved?" This from Lt. Harrington, who watched her closely.

"I'm guessing that if you have a dossier on Sgt. Martinez, then you have one on me, too," Holly said, choosing her words carefully. "If that's the case, then you know I suffered permanent nerve damage in my arm as a result of the attack on my supply convoy. Sgt. Rafferty was injured in that same battle, but he'll make a full recovery, while I'm looking at a medical discharge. I can't hold a weapon and I have no interest in a desk job. I'll be leaving the military."

She ducked her head, blinking back a sudden sting of tears. She'd known that she would likely leave the Navy, but this was the first time she'd actually allowed herself to say the words out loud. Hearing them was both terrifying and painful.

"I'm sure I don't need to tell you that fraternization is prejudicial to good order and discipline, and violates long-standing traditions of the naval service," intoned LCDR Fowler. "Even if your intention is to leave the military, that doesn't excuse or mitigate any illegal conduct."

Holly raised her chin a notch. "I understand. You do what you need to do, Lieutenant Commander, and I'll do what I need to do. Now, how can I help you with your investigation into Sgt. Martinez?"

11

THE INVESTIGATORS LEFT two hours later, and Holly stood in the front entry to the lake house and watched their car disappear down the driveway. She had told them, briefly, about the events of the previous day and of the break-in during the night, which explained the presence of the two deputies who sat in a marked patrol car by the house. The investigators had taken some notes and promised to check in with the sheriff before they left town, but otherwise had given no indication whether or not they believed those events were related to their investigation.

Holly had her own doubts, but knew the events were significant enough to warrant further investigation. If the intruder was somehow connected to Martinez—and Holly didn't see how he could be—then the Inspector General would uncover that connection.

Holly looked toward the barn. Was Shane still working on the Jeep? He hadn't returned to the house while the investigators had been there, for which she was grateful. Even if she hadn't made the unfortunate blunder about coercing Shane into a relationship, Holly was pretty sure that her feelings for him were evident whenever he was near. The investigators would only have had to see the way she looked at him to guess what was going on. For now, they were just concerned about Sgt. Martinez, and that's the way she wanted to keep it. Holly only hoped that once their investigation was complete, that they wouldn't look more closely at her and Shane.

She still couldn't quite grasp the enormity of the charges being levied against Sgt. Martinez, although it certainly wouldn't be the first time a member of the armed forces had been found guilty of such crimes. She just hadn't expected to find that going on in her own unit, with one of her own men.

Despite the warmth of the afternoon, Holly shivered. Suddenly, the woods that surrounded the lake house seemed too dark and dense, the house itself too isolated. Even the waters of the lake seemed somehow threatening. Folding her arms around herself, Holly hurried down the steps and across the sweep of lawn to the ancient shed that stood on the far side of the property, the only structure that still remained from the original homestead. Her mother had wanted it torn down and replaced with a modern garage where they could store the boat during the winter and keep the cars out of the weather, but her father had refused. Holly was glad.

Shane had opened the doors to the front of the shed, and sunlight streamed in, revealing the fully restored, WWII era Willys Jeep that had been in Holly's family for as long as she could remember. Her parents had driven that Jeep in more Fourth of July and Memorial Day parades than she could count.

Shafts of light streamed in through chinks in the

plank walls, and dust motes swirled lazily in the shifting light. Beyond the Jeep, the interior of the shed lay in shadow, but Holly could make out the shape of her father's workbench and various carpentry tools and implements hanging on the wall.

Stepping inside, she breathed in the familiar smells of her childhood—gasoline and dried grass, oil and wood shavings, and the musty smell of canvas and aged leather. A noise attracted her attention, and rounding the front of the vintage Jeep, she found Shane bent over the workbench, the muscles in his arms flexing as he manipulated something on the work surface. She stood and watched him for a moment, recalling the times he and Mitch had worked on the Jeep together. Having him at the lake house with her seemed natural, and for a moment she wished that everything could be as simple as it had been when they were younger. He turned as her shadow fell across him, and his hazel gaze swept over her in one assessing glance. Holly felt her entire body warm under his regard.

"Are you okay?"

She nodded. "Yes. Just a little creeped out. I'm glad the deputies are still here."

Shane gave a noncommittal grunt.

"I don't think the IG is interested in us, Shane," she continued after a moment. "They just want to find out what Sgt. Martinez is doing."

Leaning back against the workbench, he rubbed both hands over his face. "Holly," he groaned. "What the hell were you thinking? You told them you coerced me into sleeping with you. How do you think that sounds? Jesus, it's only a matter of time. Once they finish investigating

Martinez, then they'll start looking at us. You could be court-martialed."

"I don't think that will happen," Holly replied, running her finger along the hood of the Jeep and hoping that she sounded convincing. "Why should they care about us? They're more interested in fraternization between direct reports. We're not even in the same unit."

"Do you really want to take that chance? To have your career end in disgrace?" Turning away from her, he braced both hands on the workbench and spoke to her over his shoulder, his voice bitter. "Trust me, it's not worth it."

Holly stood uncertainly for a moment, trying to quell the panic that surged through her. She knew he referred to his own father, whose career as a horse trainer had nearly been ruined because of his relationship with Shane's mother.

"So what are you saying?" she finally asked, her heart beginning to thud hard. "That we should end this?"

Holly could almost see the muscles in his body bunch, as if he braced himself for a physical blow. "I don't know what the answer is anymore," he finally admitted. "I've spent so many years trying to do the right thing by avoiding you, but quite frankly, I don't think I can go back to that."

"Then don't." Holly stepped close to him and wrapped her arms around his waist, pressing herself against his warmth and strength. "Being with you feels right. I don't want to go back to the way things were before, either. I knew you wanted me. Even then, I knew."

She felt his body tighten and he gave a soft huff of laughter. "I tried to hide it, but you were so freaking determined to break me down."

"No," she murmured, rubbing her cheek against his back and splaying her hands across the layered muscles of his stomach. "I didn't want to break you down. I just wanted you to let me in, to let me see the real you."

"That's what I'm afraid of," he admitted huskily.

Hearing his words, Holly thought her heart might stop beating. Slowly, she took his arm and turned him to face her. His expression was shuttered and he wouldn't meet her eyes.

"You think I won't like what I see?" she asked softly.

"Holly..." His voice sounded anguished. "You could have any guy you want, and I know there were dozens at the academy who would have suited you perfectly. Guys with good names who came from old money. Guys who could give you stability. Respectability. Everything I can't." When he finally looked at her, she saw the combination of defiance and misery in his eyes. "I never understood what it was you see in me."

Holly stared at him, unsure whether to feel flattered or insulted. "What? You think that's all I care about? A guy with a pedigree and a balance sheet?"

"*You're an admiral's daughter.* Even you can't pretend that your father will be thrilled to see you hook up with me."

Holly stared at him, aghast. "Do you honestly believe that? My father has nothing against you and you know it. He's always liked you. Even when you ditched high school and joined the Marines, he never said a critical word about you. He said you'd been through some rough times, but you were a man who knew what you wanted and that you'd do okay. He believed in you, Shane, and so do I."

She thought he would push her away and say something sarcastic, the way he might have done when they were both younger. Instead, he cupped her face in his hands and kissed her.

"Thank you," he said, tipping his forehead to hers. "I don't know what I did to deserve you, but…thank you."

It wasn't a declaration of love, or even a commitment, but Holly would take it. She'd take whatever Shane had to give her and try not to want more than that. She kissed him, savoring the intensity of his response before pulling away with a breathless laugh.

"Okay, then." She peered over his shoulder. "What have you been working on down here? Is that my camera bag?" She turned to Shane with a puzzled smile. She realized she must have left it in the boat the previous day. Until that moment, she hadn't even missed it.

On the worktable itself was a set of vises, and she saw her camera had been clamped into one. She watched as he loosened the vise and removed the camera, handling it with care.

"Back on the island, I noticed that you had some trouble holding the camera with your left hand," he said quietly. "I made a modification that I think might help. Here, try this."

Holly narrowed her gaze at him, but took the camera and studied the slim bracket that he had mounted on one side of the body.

"It's nothing fancy," he said, "and it won't get in the way of changing the lens or removing the memory card, but it will allow you to hold it with your left hand without worrying that you'll drop it. Let me show you." Leaning toward her, he took her left hand and slid her fingers through the bracket so that they were tucked firmly against the body of the camera. "You see? If you tip your hand this way, the weight of the camera will hold it in place and you can use your other hand to change the lens without having to balance it on your lap."

Holly tested his theory and found that she could hold the camera securely in her left hand without having to curl her fingers around it. She raised her eyes to Shane's, hoping he didn't see how much this small gesture meant to her.

"Oh, Shane. You did this for me?" Her voice sounded small and shaky and she cleared her throat. "Thank you."

"You're welcome." He hesitated. "It's nerve damage, isn't it?"

Holly nodded. "At first the doctors thought it might be temporary, but now they believe the damage is permanent."

"Does it hurt?"

She shook her head. "Not really. My hand and fingers tingle, sort of like the pins and needles you get when your foot falls asleep. And sometimes my hand won't do what I want it to do, like grip things." She shrugged. "I'm not complaining. It could be a lot worse."

"So that's why you think you'll leave the military?"

"I *am* leaving the military. I go before the medical board in three weeks to determine if I'm fit for duty, but even if they say I can return, I don't think I will. I'm ready to get out."

Shane blew out a hard breath. "Holly, leaving the Navy isn't your only choice. There are plenty of guys with injuries worse than yours who have returned to duty."

"Yeah, to desk jobs," she said bitterly.

"Not just to desk jobs," Shane argued. "You're in the Navy and you're an officer. Your assignment in Iraq was an exception to what most Naval officers do. You could go to sea and possibly have your own command. But you're never going to do that with a defeatist attitude. Jesus, Holly. You could do anything you want."

"Maybe I *want* to leave the military."

"Then that's something entirely different."

Holly looked at him in despair. "There's a part of me that does want to leave, but I know it's going to kill my dad."

Shane gave her a tolerant look. "Now who's not giving him enough credit? He just wants you to be happy, Holly. If leaving the military will make you happy, then I'm certain he'd support your decision. But you have to leave for the right reasons."

Holly groaned in frustration. "That's just it. I've never really considered anything outside of the military. I don't have a clue what I would do. The military is all I know. But if I stay, I'll always feel like I'm not living up to my potential."

There was silence. "Jesus, Holly…"

She looked sharply at him, detecting the self-loathing in his voice. "None of this is your fault, Shane."

"You say that, but you could have been killed." His voice sounded strained.

"You very nearly were," she rejoined. "You may not remember, but I do. I was there. I saw you after the explosion, with bits of steel poking out of your body and every inch of you covered in blood. I was there when you stopped breathing and they didn't think you were going to make it." She stared at him through the dust motes. "I never want to go through anything like that ever again."

He drew in a deep breath and rolled his shoulders, as if to ease some strain. "I'm sorry you had to see that." He hesitated. "But I have to go back, you know that."

She nodded and pretended to study the workmanship on her camera, staring blindly at it. She was close to tears and even closer to begging him not to return to the military. "I know. You're a good soldier."

He dipped his head to meet her eyes. "I don't feel as if I have a choice about it, Holly. My unit needs me."

I need you.

"I understand," she said, struggling to keep her voice level. And she did understand, but that didn't mean she had to like it. But she couldn't keep talking about it, or she'd lose what little composure she had left. She turned the camera over in her hands, examining how he had fastened the bracket. "How did you learn to do this?"

Shane chuckled softly. "I'm the MacGyver of our unit. I did a lot of modifications to the armored vehicles in Iraq, and even to our personal equipment. Your dad keeps some tools out here, so I used those. It was pretty easy, actually."

"You did a great job."

"Thanks." He pushed away from the work bench and held his hand out for the camera. "I know I said we'd head back to Chatham today, but the deputies said everything has been quiet. We can stay another night, unless you'd rather not."

Holly didn't particularly want to remain at the lake house, not after what had happened the previous night, but Shane would keep her safe; she knew that. Although common sense told her it would be wiser to return to Chatham immediately, her heart couldn't resist spending one more night alone with Shane. Just one more night. With the deputies still on site, she had to believe nothing bad could happen.

"Okay." She nodded. "Another night."

"C'mon inside and I'll fix us something to eat. Just remember, you don't have to make any decisions yet. You still have a few weeks to think about it, okay?"

HOLLY PERCHED ON A STOOL at the center island and watched as Shane prepared turkey club sandwiches for both of them. He was pretty comfortable in the kitchen, having taken care of his father during those dark years after his mother had died. But his movements were automatic; he was scarcely aware of what he did.

His thoughts were on the visitors they'd had that morning, and the ongoing investigation into Sgt. Martinez's activities. There was something about the photo…he'd told the investigators that he didn't know the man, so why did he have a sinking sensation in the pit of his stomach each time he recalled that photograph? There was something there, he just couldn't put his finger on it.

"Mmm, delicious," Holly declared, finishing half of her sandwich and pushing the rest away. "I can't eat another bite."

Shane paused in the middle of taking a hefty swig from a bottle of chilled beer and frowned at her. "You're done?"

"I'm stuffed."

"You hardly touched it."

Holly laughed. "It was a huge sandwich! I'm not built like you and I don't need that much food."

Shane let his gaze drift lazily over her, taking in every curve. She was taller than most women, just a few inches shorter than himself, with long legs and an ass that had driven him nuts back when he was a teenager. He'd spent more hours than he cared to recall imagining those legs wrapped around him while he cupped her sweet ass in his hands. The reality had completely eclipsed his fantasies. Just thinking of how she'd clung to him that morning had him growing hard for her again.

"Personally, I'm glad that you're not built like me," he said, "although I don't think you eat enough. Especially considering the calories you've burned over the past couple of days."

Just like that, the atmosphere in the kitchen changed, became charged with an undercurrent of electricity. He watched with interest as warm color crept up from under the collar of her shirt and stained her neck pink.

"I could stand to lose a few pounds," she said breathlessly, her eyes fastened on him as if she expected him to pounce.

Shane pushed his empty plate to one side, silently acknowledging that he was still hungry, only not for food. "You lose any weight and I'll force feed you MREs. You're perfect."

He referred to the premade meals that the troops ate when in combat. They were designed to pack as many calories and nutrients as possible into each serving. Shane had eaten more of them during his deployments than he cared to remember.

Now he watched Holly's color deepen. He could have continued—he loved to see her flustered and unsure of herself—but stacking the dishes in the sink, he decided to give her a break. "I'm going to give the sheriff a call and see if they have any more to report on the intruder." He was actually a little irritated that he hadn't heard from the sheriff before now. He wanted to know just who the man was, and why he'd singled out the Durant house for his crimes. But what he really wanted was to find out if the guy was working alone or if, as he'd suggested, he was part of a bigger circle of thugs who had a death warrant out for Holly.

He wondered, too, if the bastard was somehow connected to the Martinez investigation, although Holly had assured him that there was no way the supply clerk could know he was being investigated. Even when Holly had requested he be moved from Al Asad Air Base to Camp Fallujah, he'd apparently been told it was just a routine rotation. In fact, Holly's commanding officer had been the one to deliver the news to him in order not to arouse his suspicions. Still, what other explanation could there be? There was something about the entire scenario that nagged at him, and it irritated and frustrated him not to be able to pinpoint it.

Shane stepped onto the deck and closed the doors behind him, unwilling for Holly to hear his conversation, and punched in the number for the sheriff.

"We still have him in custody," the sheriff reported, "but he's not talking. He has no ID on him, and he's not coming up on any of our databases."

"Give me fifteen minutes alone with the son of a bitch, and I guarantee you he'll talk," Shane all but growled into the phone.

The sheriff laughed, but even over the phone, Shane heard the uneasiness in his voice. "That may work on detainees in Iraq and Afghanistan," he said, "but it won't work here. We're going to do this the legitimate way."

Shane blew out a hard breath. "Does he have a lawyer?"

"The court will appoint a public defender for him." The sheriff paused. "We have him on breaking and entering with a dangerous weapon, but we have no evidence that he was responsible for tampering with the boat motor, or that he fired that hunting rifle."

"But you know it was him, right?" There was silence, and Shane gave a disbelieving laugh. "It had to have been him. And what about his threat of sending in more thugs to finish the job?"

"Don't get riled up, son. I'm not saying we don't have reasonable cause to put this guy away, but it may be that he's here illegally from south of the border. In which case, the court may simply decide to deport him, rather than incarcerate him."

"Deport him where? Back to Mexico?" He couldn't keep the scorn out of his voice. "Because that's not good enough, Sheriff. If he came into this country illegally once, what's to prevent him from doing it again? To my way of thinking, Mexico isn't far enough. I want this guy sent to fucking Siberia."

"I understand your frustration, I really do. We had two visitors this morning who were also interested in your intruder."

Shane knew he referred to the investigators from the Inspector General's office. "I'm guessing they didn't have any luck getting him to talk, either."

"No, but it's an interesting theory that this guy could be an accomplice to the supply clerk being investigated. If we could ID the guy, we'd know a lot more."

Shane sighed. "Okay. I'm going to bring Holly back to Chatham tomorrow morning and have her stay with her parents. But I want your assurance that you'll contact the Chatham police department and have them send a detail to cover the house."

"I'll call Chief Wright myself and have him set it up."

Shane disconnected the call, feeling more frustrated than before. He couldn't ever recall this total sense of helplessness. Not even when his dad had lost both his job and the house and had descended into a booze-sodden depression for two years. At least then, Shane had been able to do something. He'd managed to keep his father alive, and had even taken his high school GED so that social services couldn't remove him from his dad's life.

But in this case, he had no control and no influence. For the first time, he wished that he'd joined a special operations detachment, or had chosen to become an officer. At least then, he'd have some ability to collect information or to exert influence in order to get the answers he needed. But as things stood now, he was completely dependent upon whatever the sheriff chose to share with him.

He heard the door open behind him and turned to watch Holly join him on the deck. She walked past him and leaned forward to rest her elbows on the railing and stare out at the lake. "I've always loved coming out here," she said. "This has always been my happy place, where I feel most comfortable." She angled her head and looked at him over her shoulder. "Chatham is beautiful, don't get me wrong, but it always feels a little constrained. Like a corset. This place is…freedom. You can breathe here."

Shane smiled at her analogy, since he knew exactly what she meant. Even though his father had found a good job in Chatham, at one of the best stables in the county, he'd never felt completely welcomed. He knew that most of the town considered him to be little more than riffraff, and only tolerated him because his father was so gifted with horses. That was part of the reason he'd left to join the military. He couldn't stand the sidelong glances and whispered musings about his past. Only the Durants had never questioned his background, accepting him into their home without any reservations. He wondered if they would have opened their doors to him then, if they'd known how badly he'd wanted their daughter.

"You shouldn't be out here," he said darkly. "A sniper could drop you like a deer."

Holly turned and leaned against the rail and regarded him solemnly. "You don't believe this guy acted alone. You think there's someone else involved, don't you?"

Shane recalled again what the intruder had said; that there were others who would come to finish what he'd started. Had he been telling the truth, or just bluffing? He blew out a hard breath of frustration and scrubbed a hand over his hair.

"Honestly? I don't know what to think. But until we know who this guy is and what his motives are, I think we need to be practical. Now come inside."

His voice brooked no argument, and Holly didn't argue when he indicated that she should precede him back indoors. Only when the doors were locked and the blinds drawn closed did he relax a little.

"I just got off the phone with the sheriff and he said the son of a bitch isn't talking. They have no ID on him, and he doesn't show up in any of their databases. The sheriff has some reason to believe he's here illegally from Mexico, in which case the courts will probably deport him."

Holly looked puzzled. "So who is this guy? And what possible motive could he have for breaking into this house and threatening me?" She hugged herself around the middle. "It makes no sense. But you're right. I'll feel better once we're back in Chatham. I love this place, but right now it gives me the creeps."

Shane drew her into his arms and rubbed his hands over her back, relieved that she didn't argue the point. "I won't let anything happen to you."

Holly burrowed closer. "Do the police think the guy has an accomplice?"

"Yes," Shane acknowledged with reluctance. "But only because they haven't found a car or the gun used in the shooting. Until we can tie the other two incidents back to him, there's no way to guarantee he isn't working alone. I'm sorry. I know you were hoping we could stay here for three weeks, but until we get to the bottom of whatever is going on, I think we need to take a rain check."

"I'll do whatever you think is best," she assured him, hugging him. "If you think I should go home, I'll go."

Shane struggled to control his emotions. "The police in Chatham can do a better job protecting you at your parents' house than the sheriff can do here on the lake. The property is too big, too isolated."

"What will we tell my parents?"

"We'll tell them the truth. Your father will want

you under his roof." His arms tightened around her. "I couldn't live with myself if I let something happen to you. Again."

Holly was quiet for a long moment. "What about our three weeks?"

"I'll give you your three weeks," Shane promised grimly, his chin on top of her sleek head. "Maybe it'll have to be one weekend at a time, or over the course of the next year, but I promise I will give you three weeks. Hell, I'll give you all the time you want if you'll just go to Chatham."

Tipping her face up to his, Holly smiled. "That sounds suspiciously like a commitment, Sgt. Rafferty."

Shane realized she was right; he was making a commitment to her. He'd spent the past eight years trying to convince himself that he was no good for her, but being with Holly Durant felt right, like he'd finally come home. The very thought of anything happening to her made him go a little wobbly through the knees. He was crazy about her. He had been since before the night of her graduation party, and he would give his own life to keep her safe.

"I should be committed," he said wryly, "to think I can order a woman like you to do anything."

"But you could," she said softly, placing her hands on either side of his face and drawing him down for a kiss. "You might be surprised at the orders I'd be willing to follow."

Shane smiled against her mouth, acknowledging that he definitely liked the sound of *that*.

SHANE WOKE UP WITH A START, sitting bolt upright in bed with his heart slamming hard in his chest and his body soaked in sweat. For a moment, he had no idea where he was and his eyes searched wildly around the room for the source of his alarm. He cocked his head and listened, but everything was quiet. A soft breeze billowed the curtains beside the bed, and the only sounds were the nocturnal insects outside.

Beside him, Holly lay curled on her side, her mouth slightly open in sleep. Her lashes were dark crescents against her smooth cheeks. At some point after their lovemaking, she had pulled on a short nightgown, and she looked both young and innocent, as if nothing dark or ugly could disturb her slumber. Shane stared at her, but his gaze was focused inward, recalling the dream he'd had of the ambush in Iraq.

Recalling *everything*.

The memories crashed over him and as if in Technicolor detail, he replayed the horrific events. Since the day that Holly had arrived at Al Asad Air Base, he'd made it a point to know where she was at any given time. He'd lost sleep thinking about what might happen to her if he wasn't around to watch over her.

When he'd learned that Holly intended to accompany a supply convoy to Fallujah Air Base, he'd immediately volunteered to ride with the security detail. There was no way he'd have been able to remain behind and not know if she was safe. Now, with his heartbeat still uneven, he remembered why he had abandoned his turret gun, and the memory made his knees go a little weak. Yes, he'd seen Holly exit her truck and make her way alongside the convoy. He'd seen when the IED had caused the truck to explode, sending her sprawling on her face in the dirt. But what had caused him to disregard protocol and training had nothing to do with the enemy insurgents.

He had seen what nobody else had; her own guy, behind her, his automatic rifle at first aimed toward the orchard where the enemy hid. But as Holly had worked her way along the line of trucks, Sgt. Martinez had turned his weapon and aimed it at her back. Shane had seen the expression on the other man's face and had known in that instant that he intended to kill Holly. Shane hadn't had a clear shot at the bastard because Holly was directly in his line of fire, so he'd done the only thing he could; he'd leapt down from the MRAP and sprinted toward her, intent on saving her.

The rest was still a little hazy, but he was certain the bullet that had shattered Holly's arm had been delivered by Martinez. He was also certain that when that bullet had failed to kill her, the soldier had lobbed one of his own grenades, but in his panic, had seriously overthrown it. Shane had been on the perimeter of the impact zone and had suffered some serious wounds, but it could have been worse.

Both he and Holly could have been killed.

The bastard had tried to frag her, a term used when a soldier assassinated a superior officer. The most common method of fragging was with a grenade or similar device. The advantage to the killer was that he could claim the grenade had been thrown during the heat of battle and had landed too close to the victim, resulting in their "accidental" death. Or the killer could claim that another soldier had thrown the device, or even that it had been lobbed by the enemy. Since the grenade itself would be destroyed during the explosion, there was no way to trace the device back to a specific soldier. If done properly, it was the perfect crime.

Only this soldier hadn't perfected his aim, and Holly hadn't died. Shane recalled the face of the man who had broken into the lake house. There was a connection between Martinez and the intruder. He felt it in his gut. They were somehow working together in Martinez's scheme to defraud the government.

Looking at Holly as she slept, he knew what he had to do next. He'd bring Holly to her parents' house and then he'd travel to Washington and pay a visit to the Inspector General's office and make a statement about what had happened that day in Iraq. With luck, the investigators would discover a connection between Martinez and the intruder, and stop the threat to Holly once and for all.

12

IT WAS EARLY THE NEXT morning when they entered the town limits of Chatham, and passed beneath an enormous banner that stretched over the main road, suspended between two utility poles. Holly grimaced and wanted to shrink down in her seat, only that wouldn't have provided any cover either, since the Willys Jeep had no doors.

"This is beyond mortifying," she wailed softly, glancing upward at the banner as they drove beneath it.

Chatham Welcomes Lt. Holly Durant—Hometown Hero!

"Why is that mortifying to you?" Shane asked mildly, glancing over at her. With the morning sun glinting off of his sunglasses and cropped hair, he looked so masculine and handsome that Holly's breath caught in her throat.

"You're not…upset?"

He gave a philosophical shrug. "Not especially. Should I be?"

"Well, it's just that you should be on that banner, too.

After all, I wasn't the only one who fought that day. You're as much a hero as I am, probably more."

He scrutinized her from behind the glasses and then reached over and covered her hand with his. "I'm not upset. I had my own reasons for doing what I did, and I can promise you that none of them had anything to with getting my name splashed across a banner, or getting to ride through town as part of a ticker tape parade. You deserve the recognition and I understand completely why I've been left off."

Holly sharpened her gaze on him. "Is your memory coming back? Do you recall why you jumped down from your truck?"

To her surprise, he avoided looking at her. "I'm remembering some things, but not the entire sequence of events. But yes, some things are starting to come back."

"But you don't recall why you left the truck." She could see from his expression that he didn't want to discuss it, and sat back in her seat with a sigh. "It just doesn't seem fair. Maybe the town doesn't understand that you were injured trying to save *me*."

He glanced sharply at her, and Holly sensed a sudden tension in him. Then he visibly relaxed and turned his attention to the road.

"According to the reports, I abandoned my post for no valid reason and I nearly got both of us killed." He gave a rueful smile. "Not exactly the actions of a hero."

"Even so, you're a Chatham resident," Holly protested. "Even if you take me out of the equation, you still put your life on the line that day, and it only seems right that the town would recognize one of its own."

Shane laughed softly. "Trust me, sweetheart, I'm not

one of Chatham's own. I was a barely tolerated blight on the pristine surface of this town, and I have no doubt that the founding fathers breathed a sigh of relief when I left to join the military."

Holly suspected *all* the fathers in the town of Chatham had breathed a sigh of relief at Shane's departure. Most of the town had ignored the Raffertys, except for the girls, who had been fascinated by Shane's brooding good looks and refusal to acknowledge any of them. Most of them—Holly included—had taken his aloof disdain as a challenge and had done everything in their power to try and attract his attention, for all the good it had done them.

"Moving here must have been difficult for you," she murmured.

Shane shrugged. "Not really. I kept to myself."

"I remember."

They were driving through the center of town, and several people turned to stare at the vintage Jeep as they drove past. Holly recognized several of them, but didn't wave in the hopes that nobody recognized her.

"Oh my God," she groaned, as they passed the town common, where generations of Chatham men had prepared for war. The grassy area had been altered by the addition of a stage and a podium, and a dozen or more white festival tents had been set up along the length of the grassy area. The white gazebo in the center of the park also sported a banner that read *Welcome Home, Lt. Durant.*

She wanted to die.

Her actions that day in Iraq weren't worthy of so much attention. In fact, what she'd done had been based on purely selfish motives. She hadn't had a choice about saving Shane; she simply couldn't go on if anything happened to him. What other option had she had? Shane Rafferty was everything to her, and she had been incapable of standing by and letting him die.

She sighed deeply. "This is crazy. The homecoming parade isn't for another five days, and they're already setting up."

Shane arched an eyebrow at her. "That surprises you?"

"If my mother had anything to do with the planning, then I suppose not."

They drove past Benjamin's Drugstore, and Holly glanced over at Shane to see if he might want to stop, but he didn't so much as glance at the building he'd once called home.

"Are you going to see your dad while we're here?" she ventured.

"I wasn't planning on it," he replied curtly, but Holly didn't miss how his hands tightened on the steering wheel. "He's probably over at the stables and quite frankly, we don't have a lot to talk about."

"I see. Well in that case, you're welcome to stay at my parents' house while we're in town. You can take Mitch's room. I know my parents won't mind."

Shane was quiet for a long moment, as if considering her invitation. "Thanks," he finally said, "but I won't be staying that long."

Holly frowned. "Where are you going? Back to the lake house?"

He glanced over at her. "No. I have an appointment at the Navy hospital in Maryland. They're, uh, going to take a look at my leg."

Now that was a surprise. He hadn't mentioned

anything about going to Maryland, or about having his leg examined. The last she knew, he wasn't scheduled to have his cast removed for another couple of weeks.

"Is everything okay?"

"Oh, yeah," he assured her. "Everything's fine. It's just, um, a routine follow-up appointment. I'm also going to check in with my unit and find out how soon I can return to duty, provided my cast comes off on schedule."

Holly drew in a deep breath. She didn't want to think about Shane returning to active duty, especially when she knew she wouldn't be going back with him. She wouldn't wait for the medical board to make a ruling; she'd already made her decision. She would request a medical discharge and return to civilian life. Doing what, she didn't yet know.

"I see." Holly studied her hands. "How long will you be gone?"

"A couple of days, no more than that," he assured her. "I will definitely be back in time to see you ride in the parade."

Holly grimaced. "You don't have to make that kind of promise. Nobody would expect you to come, not when they can't even bring themselves to acknowledge you in the first place."

"Holly." His voice was low and insistent, forcing Holly to look at him. "I will be back."

She nodded, hating how vulnerable she felt at the thought of his leaving. She forced herself to smile. "I know you'll be back. You still owe me three weeks."

Shane chuckled and turned the Jeep onto a long driveway. "Here we are," he murmured. "Home, sweet home."

Holly's parents lived in one of the town's many Victorian-era mansions, set back from the road and partially hidden behind a line of ancient trees. Holly's mother had spent years refining the property and building a network of gardens around the graceful structure. As president of the Chatham garden club, she'd hosted innumerable brunches and teas in her gardens, and held an open house each year to showcase her antique roses and enviable assortment of plantings and flowers.

Holly's father had been assigned to numerous locations during his years in service, but Holly's mother had rarely accompanied him, preferring to stay in Chatham. Their home had been a perfect backdrop for an Admiral's wife, although as Holly recalled, her mother had spent much of her time there without the Admiral. As much as Holly respected her mother for establishing a stable life for herself and Mitch, and admired her for maintaining such a lovely home, she didn't think she could ever do the same.

Glancing at Shane, she knew that if she were married to him, she would willingly follow him to wherever his assignments took him. A home was more than just bricks and mortar, and she felt strongly that a happy marriage was predicated on being together. And if he went on deployment and she couldn't be with him, she would do whatever it took to ensure that when he did return, he'd come back to a warm and welcoming environment.

With a start, she jerked her gaze away from Shane, her heart pounding. In that instant, she realized that she wanted to marry him. What she felt had nothing to do with the girlish fantasies she'd once harbored of becoming Shane's wife and living happily ever after with him. This was deeper. This was...*more*. She wanted to spend the rest of her life with him. She wanted to be there for him, to share both the good times and bad times. She wanted to bear his children, and be the safe harbor for him to come home to each night.

She loved him.

The thought of not having him in her life caused a fist of panic to form in her chest. She didn't want to live without him.

"Hey," Shane said, pulling to a stop in the circular drive and turning off the engine. "Are you feeling okay? You have a funny look on your face."

Holly blinked and stared at him, certain he must see the truth on her face. How could he not? But when he continued to look at her with tender concern, she laughed a little unsteadily. "Yes, I think so. Something hit me."

"Want to share?" He'd turned in his seat and removed his sunglasses, and the expression in his hazel eyes was so warm and caressing that she almost blurted her secret out. Even as her lips were shaping the words, the front door of the house opened and her parents came onto the wide, covered verandah.

"Holly, how could you leave like that without saying anything?" her mother called, coming down the steps to greet them. "I was worried sick about you, and with your arm still healing…"

"She's perfectly fine, Emily," her father said, following his wife down the stairs. "You see she's with Shane."

He helped Holly climb out of the Jeep and enveloped her in a warm embrace. Holly breathed in his familiar scent, a mixture of tobacco and Old Spice aftershave.

"You okay?" he asked gruffly.

Holly nodded. "Yes. It turns out that Mitch had invited Shane to stay at the lake house. So you see, I was perfectly safe. Well, mostly anyway."

"Well, I'm glad you saw the wisdom in returning to Chatham," her mother said warmly, drawing her away from her father and bestowing a kiss on her cheek. "It's unseemly for you both to stay there without—"

"Emily," her father interjected. "They're not children anymore."

"My point exactly," she said drily.

Shane came around the hood of the Jeep, and Holly could tell that he was genuinely pleased to see her parents again.

"Shane, honey, you look so much better than you did when we saw you in the hospital last month," her mother declared, coming forward to kiss him. "Thank goodness you're okay. We were so worried."

"Yes, ma'am. Thank you, ma'am."

"It's good to see you, son," said the Admiral, leaning over to shake Shane's hand. "You had us worried there. Everything okay?"

"Yes, sir."

"And I see you brought the Willys back with you," the Admiral said, standing back to admire the Jeep. "Looks like you gave her a good spit and polish."

"Yes, sir. She runs great. I'll drive her back to the lake house whenever you'd like."

"Actually, I'm glad you brought her out. Emily and I will ride with Holly in the parade this weekend, and we'll use the Willys. We drove this Jeep in the Memorial Day parade every year when Mitch and Holly were kids, but it's been a few years since she's seen any service. It'll be like old times."

Holly tried to gauge Shane's reaction, but his expression remained friendly and interested. "That sounds great, sir."

"Well don't just stand here," Emily said, looping an arm around Holly's waist. "Come inside and I'll have Ann make us some coffee and breakfast. You both look on the thin side, if you want my opinion. We can eat in the gladiola garden. The colors are spectacular and the southern magnolia trees smell divine. Holly, I just got the pictures back that you took of my flowers last week. Honestly, darling, your talents are wasted on soldiering. Why, I'm thinking of having those photos made into a calendar. We could sell them through the garden club and make a fortune. What do you think?"

Holly allowed her mother to lead her up the steps and into the house, but was helpless to prevent looking over her shoulder at Shane. She fully expected him to be right behind her, listening to her father's stories about the Jeep. Instead, she saw him draw her father off to one side of the curved porch and access a graveled path that would take them into the gardens. With their heads bent together, they could have been sharing state secrets.

As if sensing her scrutiny, Shane glanced up and for an instant, their gazes met and held. Holly felt her chest tighten, because the expression in Shane's eyes told her that he and her father weren't exchanging pleasantries. Whatever they were discussing was serious business, and she knew he was filling the Admiral in on the events of the past day.

She dragged her gaze away and forced herself to listen to her mother's chatter about the upcoming festivities that the town was planning in her honor. But her thoughts were on Shane and his impending departure.

Her instincts told her he wasn't going to Maryland just to have his leg examined. There was something he wasn't telling her, and she intended to find out what that was.

SHANE HAD FORGOTTEN just how magnificent the Durant home was, and although he'd never been one to put much stock in material possessions, he found himself a little overwhelmed by the wealth that surrounded him. Each of the fifteen rooms brimmed with antiques and expensive artwork, and the architecture of the house itself was incomparable, with seven fireplaces, four staircases, and a stained glass window in the foyer that had been designed by Tiffany himself.

To their credit, neither Emily Durant nor the Admiral seemed overly impressed with themselves or their possessions. Emily was happiest when talking about her gardens or her most recent charity, and the Admiral's true interests lay in antique cars, golfing, and politics, not necessarily in that order.

But sitting beneath a shady pergola in the gardens, surrounded by flowers and birdsong, and eating breakfast while the Durants' housekeeper served them more coffee or cleared their dirty dishes, made him realize all over again just how disparate his own life was from Holly's. He didn't feel out of place; just the opposite, in fact. From the first day he'd met Mitch, he'd spent more time at the Durant house than he had at his own. This felt more like home to him than any other place he'd ever lived. Even when his mother had been alive and they'd lived in nice house in an upscale neighborhood, he hadn't felt as settled and relaxed as he did when he was with the Durants. There was something reassuring and almost comforting in the fact that they never changed, and were genuinely happy and comfortable in their lives.

Shane had joined the military as soon as he'd been able to, but there had been a part of him that had always looked to the future with the realization that he didn't want to remain a gunnery sergeant. He wanted more.

Over the past eight years, he'd taken steps that he hoped would improve his situation, but now he wondered if it would be enough. He'd likely never be able to offer Holly the kind of life that she'd had growing up. He had a deep-rooted fear that he could give her everything he had and still come up inadequate.

Lost in his thoughts, he glanced up and caught Holly watching him from across the table. Her lips lifted in a secret smile and he knew that she was remembering just how she'd woken him up that morning at the lake house. Quickly, before his body could react, he turned to the Admiral.

"Sir, I wonder if I could impose on you to give me a lift to the drugstore?"

Holly leaned forward. "Are you going to spend time with your dad?"

Shane averted his gaze. "Uh, no. I'm sure he's over at the stables, working. I keep my old car in the garage behind the shop and I was going to use that to drive up to Washington."

Holly frowned. "Do you mean that old Ford? Shane, it probably won't even start." She turned to her father. "Dad, let him take one of your cars. At least then I won't worry that he's broken down somewhere."

The Admiral gave a bark of laughter. "Holly, honey, what you're calling an 'old Ford' is a '65 Mustang convertible. It's a classic, and I happen to know that

Shane's father keeps it in prime condition while Shane is gone."

"He does?" Holly asked.

"He does?" Shane echoed.

The Admiral narrowed his gaze on Shane. "Son, your old man couldn't be prouder of you. He brings that Mustang out every month and drives her through town just to keep her pipes clear. If that car doesn't purr like a kitten the first time you turn her over, I'll eat my hat."

Shane felt a little stunned by the news. The few times he'd been home during the past eight years, the Mustang had surprised him by starting right up, but he'd never guessed his father had anything to do with it. Now, looking back, he wondered how he could have been so obtuse.

"I had no idea," he admitted. "I'll stop by the stables on my way out of town to say hello."

"Well, how long are you going to be gone?" Emily asked. "I hope you'll be back in time for the parade and the festivities. It just wouldn't be the same without you, Shane. Especially considering what you did to save our little girl."

"Mother," Holly protested weakly.

"I realize the Marine Corps does not view your actions in the same heroic light that we do," Emily continued quietly, "but I want you to know that the Admiral and I are grateful to you for your efforts."

"Thank you, ma'am. I appreciate that. I'll be back in just a few days," Shane assured her. What he needed to do wouldn't take that long. He pushed his chair back and stood up. "I should probably get going. If I leave now, I can be in Washington by two."

"This is all so rushed," Emily protested. "Must you

leave this instant? Why, the traffic will be horrendous." She turned to the Admiral. "Tell him to wait a few hours, at least."

The Admiral leaned back in his chair and sighed. "Son, if there's one thing I've learned during thirty years of marriage, it's not to contradict Emily." He winked at his wife to take the sting out of his words. "If I were you, I'd wait a bit."

Emily nodded in satisfaction. "You'll avoid the traffic and probably still arrive at the same time."

"I'll meet you out front in an hour," the Admiral said, standing up. "I have a few phone calls to make and then I'll drive you over to the drugstore."

"Holly, why don't you show Shane the new fishpond that we had installed last year?" suggested Emily. "I don't think he's seen it, and the black-eyed susans are in full bloom right now. After that, follow the path to the fountain, and you'll see how magnificent the lilies are this year. And I added a new bed of carnations just beyond the arbor that I believe both of you will enjoy."

"Thank you for breakfast," Shane said, and bent to kiss Emily's cheek.

He fell into step beside Holly as she made her way slowly along a garden path edged with tall boxwood.

"Did you tell my father about what happened at the lake house?" she asked.

"Yes. He's going to make some calls and have the security system changed at the house. He's also sending in a team of guys to go over the property with a fine-toothed comb to look for any other booby traps, like the one with the boat engine."

Holly nodded. "He certainly has connections, so that won't be a problem."

"Yeah."

Shane didn't tell Holly that he'd told her father the truth about what had happened that day in Iraq; that Sgt. Martinez had intended to kill his daughter on the battlefield. He'd never seen the Admiral lose his composure, and he hadn't shown any outward emotion at the news, but he'd gone very quiet and his mouth had tightened into a thin line.

"We'll get to the bottom of this," he'd promised Shane, and that had been the end of the discussion. But Shane knew that as soon as he was alone, the Admiral would be on the phone, demanding answers. In that regard, Holly was right; her father had connections.

They walked away from the main house, following the gravel paths through gardens that boasted sculptures and small benches, and under arbors that were draped with hanging flowers. Eventually, they left the cultured gardens behind and strolled into the woods at the rear of the property.

"Where are we going?" Shane laughed as they entered the cool darkness of the trees. "I don't remember there being anything out here except more trees."

"Wait and see," Holly said with a secretive smile.

Within a few minutes, they came to a stone bridge that arched over a small creek. As they crossed the bridge, Shane saw the stream fed a small pond that was surrounded by trees and lush plants. On the far side of the pond was a gazebo.

Shane whistled softly. "I definitely don't remember this."

Holly laughed. "My mother calls it her wishing pond. She says there's something magical about being out here.

She had it made a couple of years ago. This is the first time I've seen it during the summer."

Shane thought Emily's description was accurate; the pond had an almost ethereal feel to it, and the surface was thick with white lily pads.

"Come into the gazebo," Holly urged, drawing him across the bridge and down the path that led to the pond.

The entire gazebo was overgrown with climbing wisteria, which draped across the openings in purple swags. Inside the gazebo, the only view was of the pond itself, and the flowering lily pads that floated serenely on the surface.

Holly drew Shane down onto the swinging bench. "Nice, right?"

"Very nice."

"So how come you lied to me?"

Startled, Shane swung his gaze around to her. "What?"

She gave him a tolerant look. "You told me that you were going to Maryland to have your leg looked at, yet you told my parents you were going to Washington. So which is it?"

Shane backpedalled furiously. "Bethesda. Definitely Bethesda."

"I don't believe you."

Shane studied her for a moment, seeing the resolve in her eyes. "Fine. I'm not going to Bethesda. I'm going to see the Inspector General and tell them what I remember about the day of the attack."

Holly gave a small gasp and straightened. "You *do* remember what happened."

"I do." He frowned. He didn't want to tell Holly what

his memory told him was the truth. Nobody wanted to hear that someone under their own command had tried to kill them. But more than that, he knew she'd feel responsible for his own injury once he told her why he'd abandoned his post.

"Tell me what you remember," she insisted. And then, when he didn't immediately respond, "That's not a request."

Shane blew out a hard breath, finding it difficult to relive those moments. "I asked to be assigned to your convoy that day. I knew you were in the third truck and when we came under attack, I watched for you. I saw you and Martinez start to make your way alongside the vehicles." He leaned forward to brace his elbows on his knees and scrub his hands over his face, unable to continue.

Holly wanted to reach out and comfort him, but she sat frozen, her mind reeling over what he'd just said. *He'd asked to be assigned to her convoy.* The impact of that stunned her. As much as he tried to pretend he was immune to her, his actions that day said otherwise. Sucking in a deep breath, she forced herself back to the present.

"What happened then?" Holly asked softly. "I remember there was an explosion behind me, and Sgt. Martinez and I were both thrown forward."

Shane nodded, not looking at her. "Yeah. But then you got up and kept moving, while Martinez…"

"What? What did Martinez do?"

Lowering his hands, Shane angled his head to look at her. "He raised his fucking gun and pointed it right at your back."

Holly blinked. She had a difficult time reconciling

the man who Shane was describing with the man she'd known in Iraq. Martinez had always seemed so non-threatening and pathetic. She never would have guessed that he was capable of any kind of violence, never mind murder. "Oh."

"Yeah. You were right in my line of sight or I would have plugged the son of a bitch right then and there."

"But instead you left your position and tried to run to me."

"I thought if he at least saw me coming…if he knew that I knew what he was up to, that he'd back off."

Holly was staring at him now, her dark eyes huge in her pale face. "But you were shot. And I ran to help you."

"And gave Martinez the lucky break he'd been looking for. He shot you, but you didn't go down. And then he realized that I was a witness and so he threw a grenade, thinking he'd just kill us both." He gave a humorless laugh. "But he's a supply clerk and didn't have the kind of battlefield experience that the rest of us had. He seriously overthrew the grenade, which is the only reason you and I are sitting here right now."

"But why?" Holly wasn't looking at Shane. She was staring sightlessly at the pond, remembering the events of that day. "Why would he want to hurt us?"

"You were having him investigated."

Holly did look at Shane then, and he saw the confusion on her face. In her entire life, she'd never had anyone deliberately set out to hurt her, and he could see how deeply the news affected her.

"Come here," he said roughly, and drew her gently into his arms, tucking her head beneath his chin and using his good foot to set the swing into motion. "None of what happened was your fault," he assured her. "And what Martinez did wasn't even personal, as crazy as that sounds. He was panicked, knowing that he was about to be exposed as a liar and a thief."

"But that's just it," Holly said, her voice muffled against his chest. "I took care not to arouse his suspicions. He couldn't have known that I'd requested an investigation. The only person I told was my commanding officer and the Inspector General's office."

Shane stilled, and then a deep fury filled him until he had to concentrate to keep his breathing normal and his touch gentle so that Holly wouldn't guess. Holly's commanding officer was involved in whatever sleazy scheme Martinez was caught up in. He wondered if killing Holly had always been part of the plan, or if Martinez had simply grabbed the opportunity as it had arisen. For the first time, he grasped the full enormity of what had happened, and how close he'd come to losing Holly.

He pressed his mouth against her hair, loving the feel of the silky strands against his mouth, loving her fragrance, loving *her*.

"I don't want you to worry about anything," he said, his voice husky with repressed emotion. "Everything is going to be fine."

Holly nodded and wound her arms around his waist, insinuating herself closer, until she was almost sitting on his lap. "I want to go with you," she said firmly, and kissed his throat. "You'll need my testimony."

"No. You've already made your statement and told the IG everything you know. This is my statement, and it's better if I go alone." He hesitated. "We don't need to give the IG any more ammunition to use against us, and if you come with me, I don't think I'll be able to hide how I feel about you."

Holly paused in the act of tasting his skin and pulled back to look at him with an enthralled expression. "How do you feel about me?"

Shane stared into her chocolate dark eyes and knew he was lost. He had been since the day she'd walked into Benjamin's Drugstore and ordered a cherry Coke, and then drank it without once taking her eyes from him.

"I do better with hands-on demonstrations," he growled softly, and lifted her so that she straddled his thighs. Sliding his hands to her bottom, he pushed them beneath the hem of her sundress and reveled in the feel of her warm skin beneath his hands. "And I think I'm beginning to understand the benefits of wearing a dress."

Holly laughed softly and raised herself up on her knees to wind her arms around his neck and lower her mouth to his. Her lips were incredibly soft and moist and she tasted faintly of sweet melon.

"Love me before you go," she begged, her voice low and urgent against his mouth.

Without waiting for his answer, she reached down and fumbled with the fastening of his shorts. He was already hard for her, but he grasped her wrist, needing to slow her down.

"Holly, what if someone comes?"

She leaned back slightly to look at him with a crooked smile. "Well, gee, I was kind of hoping that would be me."

Shane laughed and then stopped breathing as she unsnapped his shorts and lowered his zipper, and slid her hand beneath the waistband of his boxers. He heard her breath hitch when she found him hot and hard, and that small sound was a complete turn on.

He forgot about where they were or that anyone could come across the stone bridge and find them. There was only Holly, warm and alive and vibrant in his arms. She kissed him, sliding her tongue against his as she gripped him in her hand, until sparks of white-hot lust firecrackered behind Shane's eyelids. The only thing that mattered was getting inside her as fast as possible.

Hooking his thumbs in the waistband of her panties, he dragged them down her hips, and she shifted her weight to help push them free of her body. Then there she was, pulsing and warm and soft against the part of him that ached for release. He wanted to go slow, to take his time and watch her reach her pleasure first, but he never had the chance.

Holly braced herself with one hand on his shoulder and positioned him at the entrance to her body, and then lowered herself over him in one smooth, blissful movement. Shane gritted his teeth at the exquisite sensation of sinking into her wet heat, but when she gave a deep groan of sexual pleasure and began rocking against him, he lost whatever tenuous control he'd had.

Gripping her hips in his hands, he thrust deeply and only the fact that his good foot was planted firmly on the floor of the gazebo kept the swing from rocking wildly. Even so, the rhythmic movement of her body against his was too much. He wasn't going to last, but it was okay because Holly was there too, her hands buried in his hair as she angled for deeper penetration. She clutched at him, rising over him as she used her thighs to leverage her sensual movements. She gasped and Shane swallowed her soft cries of satisfaction as a powerful orgasm gripped her, and then pulled him over the edge to join her.

Breathing heavily, he wrapped his arms around her and just held her, breathing in her scent and feeling the hard thump of her heart against his. Her arms were still wrapped around his neck and her fingers threaded idly through his hair as she struggled to catch her breath.

"Oh, man," he finally groaned. "That was unexpected."

"But amazing."

Shane laughed. "Oh, yeah…. Sweetheart, I hate to do this, but if we don't head back to the house in the next few minutes, your old man is going to come looking for us. I don't know about you, but I don't want to have to explain this to the Admiral."

Holly smiled against his neck. "Mmm, me neither."

Reluctantly, Shane eased her away from him and helped her to retrieve her panties. With their clothing back in place, they made their way out of the gazebo and back over the stone bridge. Shane kept her hand tucked loosely in his, reluctant to let her go completely.

"So, I'll call you when I get to Washington and let you know how it's going."

She nodded.

"I don't know what's going to happen. We may both have to testify, eventually."

"I don't have a problem with that. Do you?"

An image of Martinez raising his gun at Holly's unprotected back came back to Shane and he felt again that sensation of panic and desperation and utter helplessness. He curled his hand tighter around Holly's. "No, I have no problem whatsoever with it. If I have my way, he'll spend the rest of his life in Leavenworth."

They retraced their steps back toward the house until they came to a small clearing with a fountain. In the center stood a small sculpture of a cherub pouring a jug of water into the surrounding pool. Thick yew shrubs surrounded the circular fountain and ivy climbed over the carved feet of the stone benches on either side.

"I always loved this part of the garden," Holly mused. "When I was a little girl, I'd pretend I was a princess being kept in a forbidden castle against my will, waiting for my knight in shining armor to rescue me."

"And then I showed up," Shane quipped. He'd meant it as a joke, but when Holly turned to him, there was nothing remotely humorous about the expression on her face.

"Yes," she said softly, "and then you showed up. A reluctant hero who wanted nothing to do with princesses."

Shane gave a small laugh. "I don't think I'd describe you as a princess, Holly. A real princess would wait for her hero to save her, not go charging into battle to save *him*."

Holly flashed him a smile. "It seemed like a good idea at the time. I'd do it again if I had to."

"I hope it never comes to that. You've had enough close calls in the past month to last me the rest of my life." Then, afraid he'd said too much, Shane glanced toward the house. "I should get going. Your father is waiting for me."

"Come this way. My mother said there's a new garden she wants us to see."

Holly led him beyond the fountain to where the path circled toward the side of the house. In a small clearing, they saw Emily had planted red, white, and purple carnations in the pattern of the American flag.

"Very nice," Shane commented. "I can never think of your mother without thinking of flowers. Are you really going to turn your photos into a calendar?"

To his surprise, Holly blushed. "I don't know that they're good enough. Mother thinks they are, but that's not the reason I took the photos. I just thought that someone ought to capture the beauty of her gardens."

"I've seen your photos, Holly. I think your mother is right—you have a true talent with a camera. Have you ever thought of doing something professional?"

"Sometimes. But dreaming and doing are two very different things. There are a lot of talented photographers out there who've spent years perfecting their craft. I just sort of go on instinct."

"Sometimes instinct is what separates the survivors from the rest of the pack," Shane said quietly. "And you're a survivor, Holly."

She flashed him a quick smile of gratitude. "We'll see." She gestured toward the flowers. "Don't be surprised if you see these gardens all over Chatham next year."

He'd embarrassed her, but he didn't care. He knew he'd planted the seed of an idea, and that's all that mattered.

"Does the garden club usually adopt her ideas?"

"They're more like strong recommendations. In case you hadn't noticed, my mother is very determined and she usually gets her way."

"At least now I know where you get it from."

Holly laughed, but sobered almost immediately. "How long do you think you'll be gone?"

"A couple of days, max. Really," he said, noting her downcast face. "I'll call you if anything changes. The only thing you need to worry about is yourself." Stepping close, he caught her face in his hands and let his gaze drift over her features. "Promise me that you'll stay in the house. Don't go anywhere alone, even here in town. Don't let any strangers into the house, and don't go back to the lake. Got it?"

"I'll be fine. Now that my father knows what's going on, he's not about to let me do anything or go anywhere alone. In fact, he'll probably have an entire team of Navy SEALs stand guard outside my bedroom door, just as a precaution."

"Not if they know what's good for them," Shane growled. "I'm the only one who should be anywhere near your bedroom door."

Holly smiled. "Deal. Just promise that you'll be back before the parade. I've changed my mind and have decided I shouldn't have to suffer through that alone."

"I promise," Shane said, and bent his head to capture her lips with his own. For a moment, she clung to him as if she wouldn't let go. When they finally pulled apart, they were both breathless.

"I have to go," he muttered, setting her away from him.

"I know. I'll be waiting for you to come home."

Home. Until that moment, Shane would have argued that for him, there was no such place. Home was wherever his Marine Corps unit was located. Now he realized that wasn't true.

Home was wherever Holly was.

Turning, he followed the path toward the front of the house. He looked back once, briefly, to see Holly standing where he had left her against the patriotic back-drop of flowers, her fingers pressed against her mouth as if she could still feel him there. He raised his hand in farewell and then resolutely walked away.

13

THREE DAYS LATER, Shane sat outside the office of the Inspector General, where he had waited each day since he'd arrived in Washington. For an office whose mission it was to uncover criminal behavior, he hadn't had much luck in getting an appointment with any of the investigators.

He'd spoken with Holly once since he'd arrived, but hadn't told her how slow things were moving. He hadn't wanted to worry her. But when he hadn't had any luck in getting an appointment, he'd finally called the Admiral and asked for a favor. Forty minutes later, he'd received a call from the Inspector General's office, advising him to be there at 0900 the following morning. So here he waited, in full Marine dress blues, to tell his story.

The door to the office opened and a Navy Captain poked his head into the hallway. "Sgt. Rafferty."

Shane stood up and followed the officer into an office with wainscoting on the walls and gleaming cherry furniture. The Captain extended a hand to Shane.

"I'm Captain Aubrey." He indicated an upholstered chair opposite his desk. "Please, have a seat."

The Captain picked up a file from his desk and flipped it open. "I see you have eight years of distinguished service, Sergeant, and recently completed your Master's degree."

"Yes, sir." It had taken Shane the full eight years that he'd been in the service to complete his undergraduate and then his graduate degree, but he'd been determined to either move up in the military, or get out and get a job that would enable him to provide for a wife and a family.

"You're lucky to be alive. Not many soldiers can say they've survived a gunshot wound *and* a grenade."

"Yes, sir."

Captain Aubrey closed the file and set it back on his desk. "Why don't you tell me why you're here, Sergeant?"

"I'm here because I've remembered what happened that day in Iraq, when we came under attack in the Anbar Province. I know the report states that I abandoned my post and that I'm responsible for my own injuries and those of Lt. Durant's, but—"

"Lt. Durant is the female officer who risked her life to save you and was shot in the process."

"Yes, sir. Until recently, I was unable to recall the specific events of that day. I believed that I was responsible for Lt. Durant's injuries, and that may still be true, but there's additional information that I believe needs to be taken into consideration."

"Go on."

Shane related the events of that day as he remembered them, leaving nothing out. Not even the debilitating fear he'd experienced when he had seen Martinez aiming his weapon at Holly's back.

"So she did fling herself into the middle of the gun-fight to save me." Shane dropped his gaze to where he dangled his hat between his knees. "I'll have to live with that for the rest of my life. But I did see him take a shot at her as she ran toward me."

Captain Aubrey leaned forward. "Are you saying one of Lt. Durant's own men deliberately tried to kill her during the battle?"

"I'll sign a sworn statement to that effect," Shane said firmly. "Not only did he shoot her, but I believe he also threw the grenade that nearly killed us both."

"These are serious allegations, Sergeant."

"Yes, sir. I'm aware of that. But I have reason to believe that Lt. Durant's life may still be in danger."

Captain Aubrey studied Shane for a long moment before rising to his feet. "I admire your conviction, Ser-geant." Without taking his eyes from Shane, he pressed the intercom button on his phone. "Cindy, please send Harrington and Fowler into my office."

Shane gave a soft of huff of laughter and had to look quickly away at the enormous sense of relief that washed over him. The Captain believed him. That had to count for something.

The door to the office opened and the two investi-gators whom Shane had met at the lake house entered. They looked surprised to see Shane, but swiftly com-posed their features and listened as the captain told them what Shane had recalled from the battle.

"Sergeant Rafferty," LTC Fowler said, "after we were contacted by Lt. Durant regarding the allegations levied against Sergeant Martinez, we conducted an in-vestigation and discovered he was part of a widespread conspiracy of corruption that extends from some of the highest contracting officials in Iraq, to individuals in the United States acting as money brokers."

Shane frowned. "What about the guy who broke into the lake house? Is he involved in all of this?"

Aubrey leaned forward. "Martinez was flown back from Iraq earlier this week for questioning. He was a tough nut to crack, but eventually he broke down and confessed everything." He paused. "The man who broke into Lt. Durant's home is named Miguel Flores. He's a cousin of Sgt. Martinez and was apparently paid to travel to Virginia to take care of Lt. Durant."

Shane shook his head in stunned disbelief. "Why? What possible benefit could there have been for him to kill Holly?"

He realized his gaffe in calling a superior officer by her first name, but he was past caring. Even knowing the investigators would likely come after them for fraternization didn't faze him.

"Lt. Durant's commanding officer tipped Martinez off about her suspicions, but they believed she was the only person who suspected his illegal activities," Captain Aubrey continued. "Martinez thought if he got rid of her, he got rid of the only witness."

"They didn't know that Holly had also contacted your office."

"Exactly," said Lt. Harrington. "Commander Comstock never intended to contact the IG, not when he was one of the ringleaders of the whole scheme."

Shane scrubbed a hand over his face. "So how do you know there isn't someone still out there trying to kill Lt. Durant?"

"Once Martinez began talking, he dropped names fast," said Lieutenant Commander Fowler. "Commander

Comstock is being taken into custody as we speak and we believe we've rounded up all of their accomplices here in the States."

Shane sagged back in his chair. "So it's all true."

Harrington gave him a sympathetic glance. "Sgt. Martinez confessed to everything, including how he threw the grenade in an attempt to injure or kill Lt. Durant. He says he recalls aiming his weapon at her, but changed his mind when he saw you coming toward him. He said he can't recall if he actually fired his weapon or not."

Shane curled his hands into fists. "I believe he did. Maybe he panicked when I tried to intervene. Maybe, if I'd remained with my truck, he wouldn't have fired."

"Or maybe he would have fired anyway," said Captain Aubrey. "The point is, you can't second guess your actions now, Sergeant. Lt. Durant is alive, and so are you. Isn't that what really matters?"

Shane grimaced. "I'll make a full recovery, but she'll never regain full use of her arm. She believes she's no longer fit to remain in the military."

"That's a decision that only she can make."

Shane blew out a hard breath. "So what's next?"

"We'll need you to make a formal statement, and then you're free to go. We may require your testimony, but that's months down the road."

Shane rose to his feet. "Thank you. I appreciate everything you've done. Will your office contact Lt. Durant and let her know the results of your investigation? I'm sure you'll require her testimony, as well."

A touch of a smile curved Captain Aubrey's mouth. "Oh, I think we'll leave that to you, Sgt. Rafferty."

The two investigators left the office, and Shane had turned to follow them when the Captain stopped him.

"Sgt. Rafferty, if you have a minute, there's something else I'd like to discuss with you. Why don't you close the door? This could take some time."

SHANE PULLED HIS MUSTANG into the driveway of the Durant estate and shut off the engine. He was late, but he hoped not too late. He'd spent two days longer in Washington than he'd planned to, but he hoped the results would make the extra time worthwhile. Glancing at his watch, he saw it was nearly ten o'clock. He wasn't sure what time the parade started, but he'd promised Holly he would be there to support her, and he intended to keep that promise. Taking the front steps two at a time, he knocked on the door and waited impatiently. After what seemed like an eternity, the door opened and Ann, the family's housekeeper, smiled up at him.

"Why Sergeant Rafferty," she exclaimed, "don't you look dashing in your uniform!"

"Thank you." He dragged his hat from his head. "Look, ma'am, I don't want to appear rude, but I really need to see Holly. Is she home?"

"Why, no. She and the Admiral and Mrs. Durant have already left for the parade." She beamed at him. "They're riding in the antique Jeep that you drove out from the lake house, but they needed to be at Hargrave Academy early in order to line up. I understand there are a number of marching bands in the parade."

Shane tried to tamp down his impatience. "So they're gathering at Hargrave Military Academy before the start of the parade?"

"Why. yes, but they were having breakfast with the

town officials first. They left about an hour ago." Her voice dropped to a conspiratorial whisper. "Why, I heard that the Governor himself is planning to attend."

"That's great. Do you know what time the parade is due to begin?"

"Why, I believe it starts at eleven o'clock, because the speeches begin promptly at noon, followed by the barbeque on the common." Her aged face creased into a warm smile. "I've baked over a dozen pies for the occasion."

Shane smiled. "I'll be sure to try a slice of each."

Ann frowned. "The Admiral didn't believe you'd make it back in time for the parade. I think Holly thought so, too."

Shane felt his chest constrict. He'd told Holly that he would be back in time; had she given up on him so easily? He thanked Ann and turned away from the house to make his way slowly down the steps, kicking at the loose gravel in frustration. The sound of a car engine turning into the driveway made him look up in hopeful anticipation, but when he recognized his father's pickup truck, he groaned. The last person he wanted to see was James Rafferty.

He leaned against the rear quarter panel of the Mustang and waited as his father turned the engine off and climbed down from the cab of the truck. He looked tired, with lines of weariness etched around his mouth. Shane saw he wore a dress shirt and tie, and a pair of jeans that looked almost new.

"Hey, Dad," he said, keeping his arms folded across his chest. "What brings you out here?"

"I thought I saw your car over on Chalk Level Road, and I guessed you were headed here."

Shane frowned. "Why would you think that?" He hadn't told his father about his relationship with Holly; he hadn't shared anything about his life with his father in years.

"Son," his father replied, pushing his hat back on his head, "there isn't much you do that I don't know about. There never has been."

Christ. Shane fervently hoped that was an exaggeration.

"I know you think I've been a poor excuse for a father, and the truth is that I let you take on too much when you were just a boy." Removing his hat, he scrubbed a hand across the top of his head. "I depended on you for so much. Too much." He gave a self-deprecating laugh. "And you never let me down."

"Dad…" Shane didn't want to have this conversation with his father. Not now. Not ever.

"No, hear me out, son. I know you've blamed me for your mother's death all these years, but no more than I blame myself."

Shane felt his chest grow tight. "I don't want to talk about her."

"We have to talk about her, son, or we're never going to get past what happened. I loved your mother, and I couldn't imagine what it was she saw in me—a horse trainer. She could have had her pick of any fine gentleman in Lexington, but she chose me. When her parents turned their backs on her, I didn't want her to regret her decision. I tried to make her happy."

Shane narrowed his gaze. "How? By buying her stuff? Dad, I remember her crying because you were never around. You were always chasing the next Triple

Crown winner, convinced that if you could just achieve that glory, she'd finally see you were worthy of her."

His father hung his head and turned his hat around in his hands. "You're right, son. I thought if I could prove myself to her, that she'd see she made the right decision."

"But she always believed she made the right decision, dad. She loved *you*. It was always you she wanted, not the big house or the fancy address, or the fast car. Just you."

His father cleared his throat. "I see that now. But I was too young and focused on myself to realize that in trying to give her what I thought she wanted, I was letting her down."

Shane blew out a hard breath, but couldn't keep the anger or accusation out of his voice. "You left her alone all the time. Is it any wonder that she began drinking? Staying out until all hours? She gave up everything for you. You were all she had."

His father raised his head and his expression was bleaker than Shane had ever seen it. "I failed her and I failed you, but I don't want you to make the same mistake I did."

Shane thought of Holly and her privileged upbringing. But Holly wasn't like his mother; she was strong and independent. Material possessions didn't define Holly. At least, that's what Shane kept telling himself. He'd managed to save a good chunk of change in the eight years since he'd joined the military, and he could afford to buy a decent house, but he was never going to be wealthy.

"I don't intend to make the same mistakes you did," he said grimly.

His father looked away as if considering whether or not to speak, then turned back to Shane. "I've seen the way you two look at each other, son. And I've seen the way your face goes all tight whenever anyone mentions her name. I know you have feelings for Holly Durant, and you're probably thinking you're not good enough for a gal like her."

His father was right. He wasn't good enough for Holly Durant. He never would be, but fool that he was, he'd try like hell to be the man she needed.

"I'll never be able to give her this," he acknowledged, gesturing expansively toward the elegant Victorian and the surrounding gardens. "But that doesn't mean I don't have anything to offer her."

To his astonishment, his father laughed softly. "That's right, son. You have more strength and determination than any man I've ever met. You were just a kid when you left school and went to work full time to support me. How many boys could have done that?" He took a step closer. "I know you think I was too far gone to notice, but I realized the sacrifices you made for me."

"So what are you trying to say?" Shane asked.

"I'm trying to say that you already have everything that gal needs. Because all she really needs is you."

Shane drew in a slow, steadying breath. He couldn't believe this was his father talking. In the past ten years, they'd never discussed his mother, and certainly not the events leading up to her death. Now he wondered if he hadn't been too hard on his father. After all, he'd tried to give his mother everything he'd thought she needed. He just hadn't figured out that all she needed was him.

Shane looked up, surprised to find his sight a little misty. "Dad...I know I've been rough on you..."

To his surprise, his father caught him in a tight hug. "No, don't say anything else. I'm proud as hell of you, boy. I just want you to know that." Releasing Shane, he stepped back. "Now don't you have a parade to get to?"

Shane cleared his throat, which had become suspiciously tight. "Yeah. Do you, um, want to ride over with me?" He gave his father a crooked grin. "Hell, why don't you drive the Mustang? I hear you handle her pretty well."

His father chuckled. "I'd like that very much."

Shane glanced at his watch. "Well what are we waiting for? I made a promise to her, and I intend to keep it."

Shane sat in the passenger's seat and watched how his father handled the Mustang, admiring his easy confidence and control behind the wheel. Most of the main roads into town had already been barricaded to traffic, but his father took several creative detours and within minutes, they were pulling into the parking lot of Hargrave Military Academy.

Shane barely waited for the car to roll to a stop before he climbed out with a hurried thanks. The lot was congested with traffic that included military and police vehicles, fire engines, several floats, Clydesdale horses pulling a beer wagon, and what looked like the entire southern Virginia 4-H club. He dodged in between the vehicles and the people as quickly as his cast would permit, his eyes scanning the crowds until he found what he was looking for.

A 1944 Willys Jeep.

The Admiral sat behind the wheel with Emily in the passenger seat and behind them, perched on the back of the rear seat, was Holly. Like himself, she was in full dress uniform, and Shane thought she looked both nervous and unhappy, although she smiled at those who came to wish her well and shake her hand. An enormous wreath adorned the front bumper of the Jeep, made of red, white, and purple carnations.

Sidestepping around two drummers, Shane made his way over to the Jeep and leaned on the wheel well, smiling into Holly's astonished face.

"I said I'd be here, didn't I?" he asked, out of breath.

"Shane!" Holly devoured him with her eyes, a slow smile spread over her face and Shane thought he'd never seen anything quite as beautiful. "I knew you'd make it."

The Admiral turned in his seat. "Son, I suggest you climb in, or you're going to end up getting left behind."

"Oh, no," he protested. "I'm not riding in the parade. I just came by to wish you luck."

But Holly scooted over on the seat and caught him by the arm. "No, you have to ride with me."

"Holly…"

"That's an order, Sergeant," she said softly.

The Admiral chuckled. "I'd do it if I were you."

Frowning, Shane climbed into the back of the Jeep and sat next to Holly as the Admiral threw the vehicle into gear and began to slowly move out of the parking lot and onto the main road.

"This isn't right," Shane muttered. "This is your day, and I don't want to take away from it."

"You're not," Holly assured him, and laced her fingers through his. "You're exactly where you're supposed to be."

The Jeep turned the corner onto Main Street, and for the first time, Shane saw the enormous banner that spanned the road overhead.

Welcome Home Lt. Durant & Sgt. Rafferty
Chatham's Hometown Heroes

He twisted to look at Holly, knowing his face showed his confusion. "What is this?"

"While you were in Washington, I had a call from the Inspector General, confirming what really happened to my daughter that day in Iraq," the Admiral said over his shoulder, keeping one eye on the road. "Son, if you hadn't risked your life to protect Holly, she might not be alive today."

Emily turned in her seat and smiled at him. "All it took was one call to have those banners changed. They should have included your name from the first day they were raised."

Shane looked away, both embarrassed and touched by the gesture. "Thank you, ma'am," he said gruffly. "I don't know what to say."

"You don't have to say anything." Holly leaned against him to speak into his ear. "But if you don't smile and wave at these people, they're going to believe you really are one bad-assed solider."

Shane chuckled. "I'm not?"

"Not from where I'm sitting."

He smiled. "I'll have to work on that. Can't have you thinking I've gone soft."

Holly burst out laughing.

HOURS LATER, AFTER the speeches and the presentations, after the barbeque and the festivities, Shane held Holly loosely in his arms as they danced under the stars to the music of a country band. Shane had never felt as humbled as he had by the well wishes of the people who had come up to shake his hand and thank him for his service. During his adolescence, he'd resented living in Chatham and had never felt that he belonged in the upscale community. For the first time, he felt that perhaps he could live here, maybe even raise a family here.

Holly tipped her head back to look at him. "What are you thinking about?"

"My future."

He saw the quick flash of anxiety in her eyes, but she quickly masked it and smiled at him. "And what does your future hold?"

He let his gaze drift over her face, lingering on her full lips. "You, I hope."

She smiled tremulously. "Yes, I hope so, too. What else?"

"I'd like to finish out my career with the military."

She focused on one of the buttons on his jacket. To her credit, she didn't protest. "I understand. You're a good soldier. It only makes sense."

"I'll make a better officer."

Holly's gaze jerked upward. "What?"

Shane couldn't prevent the grin that spread across his face. "I finished my master's degree last year and have been playing with the idea of entering Officer's Candidate School. I met with Captain Aubrey in Washington about the investigation and after we talked, he told me that he'd read my file and thought I would make an excellent candidate."

Holly gave a bark of stunned laughter. "He's right. You would. *Absolutely.* I can't believe I never knew you were taking graduate-level courses. You never even finished high school."

"I didn't have a choice about that," he said drily. "My dad needed me and I needed to keep a roof over our heads. I took my GED when I was seventeen and began taking college level courses whenever I could."

"But don't you see? You did have a choice, Shane. And you chose to keep what was left of your family together, even though it meant sacrificing your own dreams. I'm not sure many teenagers would have done what you did."

"He was my father, no matter what I thought about him. I knew my mother wouldn't have wanted me to abandon him, but I'll admit that thought did cross my mind."

"You're not the kind of guy to turn your back on someone who needs you. You never have been."

He slanted her a doubtful look, but couldn't prevent a small smile from curving his mouth. "You've always had an unrealistically high opinion of me."

"Lieutenant Rafferty," Holly mused, ignoring his remark. "I like the sound of that." She slanted him a suspicious look. "Does this mean you'll be the one is-suing orders?"

Shane laughed. "You bet. But I can also promise that you'll enjoy following them."

"I'm leaving the military," she retorted, "so I won't have to follow them."

"You're sure about that?" Shane pulled back to look at her. "Your arm shouldn't prevent you from doing what you love."

She made a face. "I'm not sure the Navy is what I love. I don't regret the time I've served, and I've learned a lot about myself because of the military. But do I love it?" She smiled. "I love that it brought me closer to you, but I think I'd really like to settle into civilian life. Maybe I'll try my hand at photography."

"Oh, yeah?"

"I love photography."

Shane laughed. "You don't have to convince me. I'm still traumatized by the memory of you following me around with that damned camera. I think it sounds like a great idea."

"Mmm-hmm. I think so, too."

Tightening his arms around her, he drew her head back to his shoulder. "I just can't believe how this all turned out. Five weeks ago, I thought I'd lost you."

"Crazy man. You were the reason I chose to go to Iraq in the first place. You didn't think I was going to let you get away so easily, did you?"

"You were almost killed because of me." He couldn't keep the torment out of his voice. "I'll be honest with you. I feel like a fraud accepting any kind of recognition for what I did that day."

Holly pulled back and looked at him, surprised. "Why?"

"Because what most people don't know is that I'm not a hero. I did what I did because I'm in love with you. I think I have been since the first day that I saw you. I never had a choice about trying to save you."

Holly laughed softly and wound her arms around him, uncaring of who watched them. "That's where you're wrong. You always had a choice. And that's what makes you a hero."

* * * * *

COMING NEXT MONTH

Available February 22, 2011

#597 FACE-OFF
Encounters
Nancy Warren

#598 IN THE LINE OF FIRE
Uniformly Hot!
Jennifer LaBrecque

#599 IN GOOD HANDS
Kathy Lyons

#600 INEVITABLE
Forbidden Fantasies
Michelle Rowen

#601 HIGH OCTANE
Texas Hotzone
Lisa Renee Jones

#602 PRIMAL CALLING
Jillian Burns

REQUEST YOUR FREE BOOKS!
2 FREE NOVELS PLUS 2 FREE GIFTS!

♦Harlequin· *Blaze*™

red-hot reads!

JEMIMA yanked open a drawer in the sideboard to find Alfie's birth certificate. Her son was her husband's child. It was a question of telling the truth whether she liked it or not. She extended the certificate to Alejandro.

"This has to be nonsense," Alejandro asserted.

"Well, if you can find some other way of explaining how I managed to give birth by that date and Alfie not be yours, I'd like to hear it," Jemima challenged.

Alejandro glanced up, golden eyes bright as blades and as dangerous. "All this proves is that you must still have been pregnant when you walked out on our marriage. It does not automatically follow that the child is mine."

"'I know it doesn't suit you to hear this news now and I really didn't want to tell you. But I can't lie to you about it. Someday Alfie may want to look you up and get acquainted."

"If what you have just told me is the truth, if that little boy does prove to be mine, it was vindictive and extremely selfish of you to leave me in ignorance!"

Jemima paled. "When I left you, I had no idea that I was still pregnant."

"Two years is a long period of time, yet you made no attempt to inform me that I might be a father. I will want DNA tests to confirm your claim before I make any decision about what I want to do."

"Do as you like," she told him curtly. "*I* know who Alfie's father is and there has never been any doubt of his identity."

"I will make arrangements for the tests to be carried out and I will see you again when the result is available," Alejandro drawled with lashings of dark Spanish masculine reserve.

"I'll contact a solicitor and start the divorce," Jemima proffered in turn.

Alejandro's eyes narrowed in a piercing scrutiny that made her uncomfortable. "It would be foolish to do anything before we have that DNA result."

"I disagree," Jemima flashed back. "I should have applied for a divorce the minute I left you!"

Alejandro quirked an ebony brow. "And why didn't you?"

Jemima dealt him a fulminating glance but said nothing, merely moving past him to open her front door in a blunt invitation for him to leave.

"I'll be in touch," he delivered on the doorstep.

What is Alejandro's next move? Perhaps rekindling their marriage is the only solution! But will Jemima agree?

Find out in Lynne Graham's
exciting new romance
JEMIMA'S SECRET

Available March 2011
from Harlequin Presents®.

Start your Best Body today with these top 3 nutrition tips!

1. **SHOP THE PERIMETER OF THE GROCERY STORE:** The good stuff—fruits, veggies, lean proteins and dairy—always line the outer edges of the store. When you veer into the center aisles, you enter the temptation zone, where the unhealthy foods live.

2. **WATCH PORTION SIZES:** Most portion sizes in restaurants are nearly twice the size of a true serving and at home, it's easy to "clean your plate." Use these easy serving guidelines:
   - Protein: the palm of your hand
   - Grains or Fruit: a cup of your hand
   - Veggies: the palm of two open hands

3. **USE THE RAINBOW RULE FOR PRODUCE:** Your produce drawers should be filled with every color of fruits and vegetables. The greater the variety, the more vitamins and other nutrients you add to your diet.

Find these and many more helpful tips in

YOUR BEST BODY NOW
by
TOSCA RENO
WITH STACY BAKER

Bestselling Author of
THE EAT-CLEAN DIET®

Available wherever books are sold!

HARLEQUIN *Presents*

USA TODAY *Bestselling Author*

Lynne Graham

is back with her most exciting trilogy yet!

SECRETLY PREGNANT
CONVENIENTLY WED

Jemima, Flora and Jess aren't looking for love,
but all have babies very much in mind...and they may
just get their wish and more with the wealthiest, most
handsome and impossibly arrogant men in Europe!

Coming March 2011

JEMIMA'S SECRET

Alejandro Navarro Vasquez has long desired vengeance after
his wife, Jemima, betrayed him. When he discovers the
whereabouts of his runaway wife—and that she has a two-
year-old son—Alejandro is determined to settle the score....

FLORA'S DEFIANCE (April 2011)
JESS'S PROMISE (May 2011)

Available exclusively from Harlequin Presents.